THERE HAS TO BE A KNIFE

THERE HAS TO BE A KNIFE

ADNAN KHAN

ARSENAL PULP PRESS VANCOUVER

THERE HAS TO BE A KNIFE

ARSENAL PULP PRESS
Suite 202 – 211 East Georgia St.
Vancouver, BC V6A 1Z6
Canada
arsenalpulp.com

The publisher gratefully acknowledges the support of the Canada Council for the Arts and the British Columbia Arts Council for its publishing program, and the Government of Canada, and the Government of British Columbia (through the Book Publishing Tax Credit Program), for its publishing activities.

The author is thankful for the support of the Toronto Arts Council and the Ontario Arts Council.

Arsenal Pulp Press acknowledges the xʷməθkʷəy̓əm (Musqueam), Sḵwx̱wú7mesh (Squamish), and səl̓ilwətaʔɬ (Tsleil-Waututh) Nations, speakers of Hul'q'umi'num'/Halq'eméylem/hən̓q̓əmin̓əm̓ and custodians of the traditional, ancestral, and unceded territories where our office is located. We pay respect to their histories, traditions, and continuous living cultures and commit to accountability, respectful relations, and friendship.

Cover and text design by Oliver McPartlin
Edited by Shirarose Wilensky
Proofread by Alison Strobel

Printed and bound in Canada

Library and Archives Canada Cataloguing in Publication:
Title: There has to be a knife / Adnan Khan.
Names: Khan, Adnan, 1987– author.
Identifiers: Canadiana (print) 2019011925X | Canadiana (ebook) 20190119268 | ISBN 9781551527857 (softcover) | ISBN 9781551527864 (HTML)
Classification: LCC PS8621.H34 T54 2019 | DDC C813/.6—dc23

I try to catch the knife after it slips off the counter; the handle hits my shoe and the blade clatters.

You just tried to catch that? Really?

Me and Harley stare at it. It could have sliced my hand open.

You have to clean that, Omar, before you use it.

Yes, Chef.

When my cell rings, I'm thinking of Anna in our apartment, slicing onions faster than me. She would refuse to open a window or try any of the tricks you can google to stop the tears. Instead, she would slice the white vegetable, cry, and then come sobbing into the living room, pretending that I had said something horrible to her. She would do this every time she cut onions: it became our dinnertime routine that I was an inconsiderate monster.

Hello? Who is this?

It's Bernie.

What?

Bernie. Anna's father.

What do you want?

Melissa eyes me and I press the cellphone against my earskin to hear better. I move away from the pans and look at her. Red paint blisters off the kitchen walls. She's too mean for her bright blue dress, death blonde bob, and wet-black stockings. Harley says she's too old to order us around from the tip of the kitchen. She never wears her apron. He watches her with thirst. Grappa's is probably going to close soon—we never have enough customers, but it always feels too busy. Pay is one week late—pay is cash in hand—and Melissa keeps promising that it's coming tomorrow,

tomorrow tomorrow, I promise the money is there. I shrug my shoulders and move to the back.

Yo Harley, finish that for me.

Why would Anna's father call?

Are you free?

I'm at work.

Can we talk?

What do you want?

Are you free?

I'm on break.

I need something from you.

For what?

Anna died last night.

What does that mean?

Anna passed away yesterday.

I say nothing.

Can we talk?

What do you mean died? How did she die?

She passed away, Omar.

From what?

She killed herself.

From what?

What?

What are you talking about? What do you mean she killed herself?

I—

Yo Bernie, what?

Did you know that she—

What are you saying? What are you saying?

I know you broke up.

We broke up like a year ago. A year ago. Why are you calling me! Why are you calling me to tell me this? She broke up with me—why are you calling me to tell me this?

I'm sorry, please—you had to have known something?

My body lurches away from me. I hang up the phone. My mind stays with the call, but my body moves out the back door, away from the noise of the kitchen.

Look at the snow: the way it's falling to the ground, as if God had ordered it to march.

I slept like a cracked egg last night. A slug joint brought me sleep. I crumbled together three roaches and gulped the smoke down; it left me like a ghost.

She asked me out when we were sixteen. I told her I loved her in the basement of a friend's house. His parents were upstairs baking french fries with shredded cheese and gravy. Scott in the den, *Jeopardy!* on, Anna's friend lying with him, and he told me later that he had fingered her for the first time, surprised at how warm everything was, how the smell stayed on his fingers, and how his first instinct was to lick them: the taste was nothing, but her eyes went wide—she couldn't believe he would taste her like that.

We were sitting next to each other in the hall with warm coolers. She said it back, three times in a row. Ten years we strung together. She always said it like that: I love you I love you I love you.

It's Sunday and I have no work. The memory of a cigarette

starts crawling up my throat even though I'm on eight months of quitting, but, no money, so I do twenty-five push-ups instead. I'll steal one of Nathan's beers later. Light leaks onto the floor from my one window cradled in the corner of my room.

My phone is blowing up—condolences. It's on Facebook. Every time my cell dings, I look at it, read the name, but don't read the message. No calls.

Famous among my friends:

We're not breaking up! Omar, we're not, like, fucking ending forever. You're always going to be a part of me.

We had broken up, off and on, away from each other, rolling back, so many times over ten years. I don't know how many actual days we were together—only that she was there, always, even if we didn't speak.

We had really committed to our breakup six months ago and hadn't spoken in four—our longest stretch.

I do thirty jumping jacks and a sweat stain like a squid appears on my boxers. I open the window. The snow is staying on the ground for the first time this year. I take a red dress she left from the closet and sit with it on my lap, staring through the window, allowing the wind to pull into the room. I realize that my sweat will mingle with whatever smell of hers is left. I let it happen. When we broke up that last time I felt like I had misplaced something small but vital, like a set of keys, something that was mine.

I called my parents three times last night and they never picked up. They didn't really know her, but they knew about her, and I wanted to talk about the idea of her with someone, even if it had to be them. I let the phone ring forever, until I remembered that they had stopped paying for voice mail. They still pay for call display, though.

I know it's Matthew knocking on the door. I ignore it. Nathan finally lets him in.

You a'ight?

Why?

I know this is hard.

What is?

Don't be a retard.

Okay.

I'm here for you. He puts his hand on my shoulder. You're my boy. Neither of us has ever done this, and I think of the movies we've seen and how that's where we're getting our lessons from.

He runs his hand over his head, the bristles making a short popping noise. He's about three shades darker than me; his bright blue hoodie works on him in a way it couldn't on me. He pulls it off and I see his post-university health-kick muscles squeezing out of his wifebeater, like smooth rocks have been slid under his skin.

Put this on.

Nah.

Yo, it's one, get dressed. Let's get murked.

I look at his Timbs and I know he cleans them every night. He follows my gaze to his shoes and eyes them anxiously. Twice, white girls from small towns have thought he was black and targeted him for that; he went along until they fucked and then taught them about Madras.

Intelligence when drunk: there is vomit, but it's in a plastic bag.

I had become used to that wandering worrying shame after blacking out. With Matthew in the room I don't think too much; still, I scroll quickly through last night's memories trying to figure out if I embarrassed myself. We spent the day in his apartment and then the evening at Get Well until I couldn't walk. I tried to talk to two white dudes at the bar about the arcade machines that were pressed up against the wall, but I don't remember the outcome. Matthew led us back home—he is next to me now, a comma of white-yellow vomit on the inside of his wrist, his breathing shallow. I want to stretch out, so I move off my bed and onto the floor, taking a blanket, leaving him the pillow.

Yo, hmm.

What up?

What you got for breakfast?

Nothing.

Nothing?

Nathan has eggs.

How many?

I dunno. I think I heard him and his girl last night.

Man, you didn't hear nothing except you vomiting.

That's your vomit, not my vomit.

Where is it? Is it on your floor?

Nah. I got you a bag.

How you feeling?

Fine. I got some Advil.

Not your head.

Your stomach must be rough.

How you feeling about—

About what?

Don't be dumb.

Why don't you mind your own business?

Who you going to the viewing with?

You going to pick me up, right?

My room is unfamiliar to me this morning. I've lost the words for simple things: the doorknob is a blob of yellow metal, the door a weak rectangle of cheap wood, my blanket scratchy, itchy, flattened cloth trapping heat on my body. My brain struggles for grip. I'm too scared to think of Anna. When I look at the pile of books on my desk my mind scrambles to locate the word for them—books kitabs livres. Matthew watches me yank open my drawer for a joint and tells me, unhelpfully, that we smoked it all last night. I groan and lie back on the floor. I can do this. I can power through this. My cellphone is in my pocket and I delete her number from it. I regret it so fast I almost laugh—I don't have her number memorized. That's okay. I have a shift later; if I yell at someone I'll forget all about this. I focus on the nausea speaking in my stomach.

Man, you were gone last night. Matthew laughs when he says this, huddling his face into the pillow.

I remember running into Jennifer at Get Well. She worked as a hostess at Grappa's for a minute, functioning as the Korean authenticity of the place. We slept together seven times in two weeks before she left to go back to school, and neither of us has texted for the last two months. She was studying to be a nurse and spoke in complete sentences and nothing about the body disgusted her. I was hunched over her our first time together, squeezing my soft, beer-addled dick, begging it to take shape, pumping, tightening, spitting, cajoling, pinching, all while running through a catalogue of memories, from both real life and the internet, and Jennifer watched patiently. She was on her back, her breasts flattened, and working her own fingers with greater success on her clit; I realized I barely knew how my body worked. I was desperate, breathing in and out crazy, seemingly taking longer breaths in than out, which I think is not possible, flicking sweat onto her body. An impossible gap—me standing at the edge of the bed, strangling my dick, the cool air between us, Jennifer, seemingly wet, looking straight at my heaving body; our mutual drunkenness saved me from embarrassment.

Somehow, mostly soft, I was almost ready to cum. My dick was not this thing that would listen; it grew from me and was impervious to anything my mind said. Jennifer began moaning and seemed like she was about to cum, and who could blame her, and even though my half-mast cock seemed like it could spurt out a nut, I didn't want to, as this was our first time and would set the foundation for us, and, also, well, I wanted to fuck her. She moaned in an unreal way, closed her eyes, and looked away. Who could blame her? I was dripping in sweat in that hot room, my sparse chest hair matted. If I lay on her it would be like flopping a warm, wet towel onto a person. She opened her eyes again and opened her legs wide for me and I could see wetness. I turned the lamp off. It was the only light. In the dark I felt comfortable. She could no longer see the sheen of sweat that covered me like Saran wrap. The moonlight was a little slice, and I felt cooler, protected. I slowed my hand down and my mind caught onto a memory of a female shopper I had seen once, at Home Depot, the side of her breast visible, and I circled this memory, like water down a drain, until my dick began to harden.

The thought doubled over, and my awareness of jerking off in a dark room to an unaffiliated memory made me feel like a pervert and I began to lose the hard-on once more. A condom would deflate me, and having a dick just hard enough to squirm into a body, I leaned forward and told Jennifer basically that. She stopped her hand and yanked me in. I could not see her face.

My heart! It was pushing against my skin, threatening to tear. My dick hardened fully in her, and I felt like a thief for managing to make something out of this.

The sex was silent and she told me not to cum in her, directing me to her stomach, where my cum pooled shamelessly. Not totally silent: she had moaned, once, twice, encouragement when I said I was going to cum, and I basically barked in response. I had no towels so wiped her with an old gym shirt that needed washing. I sat at the edge of the bed, nervous I had not used a condom, but she didn't say anything. She drank water from a bottle in her gigantic purse, kissed me, dressed, kissed me again, and left.

I passed out and in the morning woke up with excitement, some disbelief, a memory rattled because of adrenaline but with all the important bits already coalescing into a victorious narrative. The excitement was on the verge of shame, and so it was potent—I had rescued a situation. My body was known to me and functioning. It could be trusted.

I didn't want the feelings to disappear, but they always did, futile, and like Anna, the harder I tried to force them into a shape, the more they avoided my grasp. The more I recalled them, the more I realized I was moving away from their original, pure form. The more I thought about them, the more I changed them, added details. I don't know if that Home Depot girl was the trigger—why would Jennifer's body, long, shaved, splayed in front of me, not be enough? Nerves were there, but a deep breath, and the newness was usually enough to rattle them out.

I don't know if it's the hangover, or Bernie's phone call, but it's as if I've been split into two separate things, one side only capable of looking at the other half.

We've started lunch at Grappa's to make some money—you can see on Melissa's face that the restaurant is about to flatline. All her sentences come out furious. She wears jeans in the afternoon and plays host. Different waiters wearing casual dress, dark jeans, dark T-shirts, zipping around pale and fat businessmen. The price point is like dinner's—seventeen bucks for a burger. New waiters, but me and Harley still around, his dreadlocks tied in a bun, his pasty skin covered in burn marks. He's done what I always ask him not to do: halfway cook a dozen burgers and stack them on the side of the grill, ready to go for the rush. I can see all their juice leaking out.

Where it's not that hot, trust me, brother, trust me trust me. What'd you do last night? Did your girl come around? When are you going to bring her here?

I tell him to throw the burgers out. No one wants to eat a dry-ass fucking hamburger, Harley.

I'm on salads for the rush and pans too, to fry up the chicken breasts most customers order on the side. Sachiv has soaked the floor already; he has carpal tunnel from working in a library in Sri Lanka. He works hard, with little precision, pretty perfect for a dishwasher, but sometimes the floor gets wet.

Four of my dishes are sent back because who knows why. One of them is a complaint about uncooked chicken and we stand around the plate under the brightest bulb and slice open the fattest piece of meat to look for pink.

Everything is pink on the inside, Harley says, even you two. His rocket-ship grin.

Today is slow enough that we don't need an expo: Donny is working the pass. He works the pass mostly to talk to the waitresses. We've known each other for seven years and have never had a beer outside of work.

What's wrong?

Nothing.

Four dishes back?

I don't know. I got drunk last night.

This is a lot, dude. A lot a lot.

Does Melissa know?

Not yet—but the waiters ...

Fuck them, fuck her. She owes me money.

You get back with Anna?

Nah.

How long has it been since you broke up?

Enough time.

Look at her. He points to Cheryl slicing limes at the bar. She licks juice off her fingers and has a nose like a fishing hook. Imagine that nose sniffing you. Do you know how nice her feet are? Donny views everything through this great prism of feet. Well-kept feet are the hardest thing to maintain: Do you know how much a woman must care to have nice feet? Do you know what it means to lick a hard-working woman's foot? Do you know what it means for Cheryl, working on her feet all day, to make sure they look so edible for me every night? She's never told me she loves me—but those toes, they do. Donny adjusts his dick and asks me if I've had that kind of love.

Let me get two days off next week. Thursday and Friday.

For what?

A family friend died.

Yeah, sure, man.

Donny tells me about the restaurant he wants to open, that he thinks what rich Toronto people really like is shitty food made special: Gourmet grilled cheese. Lamb meat hamburgers with processed cheese, but you gotta have that nice bread and pickles. You gotta serve it on tiny plates. White, tight, tiny plates.

Don't think about her, Matthew told me after we broke up. Pretend that she doesn't exist. Forget that you knew her. Almost everything I did had a memory that could be traced back to Anna. It's your job to forget. To pretend like it didn't happen. We would drink and drink and talk about the women in front of me now and all the life experiences I had in front of me free of Anna's complexity. Matthew would remind me: you never have to deal with late-night phone calls no more, you don't have to deal with her turnt at three a.m. banging on your door, you don't have to get screamed at in the Gap. This boots up my memory; that getting yelled at was slightly, maybe my fault—I shouldn't shoplift while she shops. I keep remembering stupid things, like when she spent two bills on a blistering orange Crock-Pot that I never used. What would happen if I looked at it again—I only saw it once before putting it away; it had really only been touched by her. I worry that my memories will be like the pages of a book, turning brittle with each turn, eventually falling apart after too much use.

Snow in the park sleeps on quiet trees. During the summer you can see hawks here. You know a predator has arrived when seagulls and pigeons burst away from the ground. How monumental is a person that you have to forget their meaning to you after you break up? Is it an insult or praise that I didn't speak to Anna for the last four months of her life, that I never called her or emailed her, that I began to parse her from my memories? I would walk by the coffee shop she worked at every day, on purpose, igniting the pain of memory, until it became less and less, until I associated the man selling books on the corner with the shop and not her. Every day I would look at him and try to memorize the books and see which ones had been sold, and maybe it worked—maybe the pain became a little less, but she was always there, lingering in the background, her memory bolted into my brain. Today when I walked past the café, it beckoned like a tomb. I asked Matthew last night: What if I knew that she was going to kill herself? What if I knew and didn't tell myself? He said with a blank face:

Did you? His eyes get watery when he drinks too quickly. I feel unhinged, like one of those solitary hawks swirling over the park.

The cold air helps me concentrate. I focus on rewriting the memories, which has become its own habit that I'll have to forget. She's going to have to occupy a different space; you're not supposed to forget the dead. I focus on my hands and bare knuckles. The dry skin. Anna loved to trace the cracks and the way my skin turned white in neat lines on the sides of my hands. Look! We're the same. She would shove our fists together. I would moisturize my skin to show her we were different.

To my left I see some people that we knew together—people that might not know she's dead yet. I am still with her until everybody knows. There are packets of memory untouched.

Peter and Jenny, with their little mutts, Crosby and Malkin. What dumb-looking dogs. I once saw Malkin lick a lid of sour cream, and seeing the dog again crackles the sour receptors of my tongue. They yell out for me with big white smiles, their breath exploding into the air. Omar Omar Omar! A siren. They don't know anything—

They are so happy they make me want to vanish. Jenny opens her body up for a hug, but my body language is so twisted that she short-circuits and instead puts a hand on my shoulder. I give Peter a handshake and then give Jenny a hug anyway. She smells like plums.

We had met them drunk at a party and ended up arranging a couple's day at a spa: Anna and Peter in the hot tub, and me and Jenny on the other side, in the sauna, the walls wet and us naked under the towels and understanding the simplicity of that and the sweaty walls mimicking our lust. Our skin had a just-fucked sheen and it was simple things like this that showed me we would work: it looked like I had a body that would fit perfectly into hers and our noses would touch naturally if I lay on her. We sweat and we sweat, and Jenny moved her legs open and closed, wanting the heat to touch her in waves. She had a birthmark like a cluster of grapes on her thigh and whenever she opened her legs I spotted it, a forever bruise. After, at the bar, she had lipstick on her teeth and I wiped it away, my thumb in her warm mouth. She thanked me and went into the bathroom to piss. I went in after she came out, the toilet paper all gone, graffiti on the walls, and her perfume searing the air.

We haven't seen you in ages! Are you okay after everything? She touches me on the shoulder.

You know—it happens.

Sure does, buddy. Do you need anything?

No.

I mean, it's been a while, right? Six months? A year?

Peter, don't be a jerk.

I'm sorry.

No, no, it's all good—he's right. I'm okay.

Are you guys still talking or anything?

I saw her last night.

Aw, that's so good. That's so good. I love hearing that.

She's amazing. If I bundle this lie in truth—she *is* amazing—then I can be forgiven. Is Allah over me in the sky, sitting on a throne on a cloud, tsk-tsking? It doesn't matter.

You guys were good together.

Peter.

Sorry!

It's okay. Really. She's gearing up for that Habitat for Humanity, you know.

Oh, that's amazing. Jenny touches me on the shoulder. She told me she wanted to open a little bar in Thailand—in Pai.

She did? My voice lilts up because I'm actually surprised. I didn't expect the Habitat for Humanity thing to land so well.

Ladyboys!

Peter, stop.

Did Anna lie to Jenny? She never told me about Thailand. What happens to dreams when you die? Can I go to Thailand for her? I know if I dream about her, she will feel alive, she will be alive in the dream—isn't that just as good?

I loved her.

Of course you did, Omar. Jenny gives me another hug. It's different now. Morphed. You can still have that love—you know, friendship. It's only a little different.

And you never know, Peter winks at me, that makeup sex! It's almost worth the breakup!

A lie is okay when it's a version of history. I excuse myself before the conversation catches me in a trap. The snow is like an exhausted star coming undone.

Peter and Jenny squabbled over their bill that day, dividing it to the last orange juice, and Anna said let's never be like them, but let's always be like them—let's get dogs and bore everyone but ourselves and let's fight over the dishes and let's only live for each other. She rubbed her nose against mine and asked if we could live like that, like two deep, pitch-black tunnels, allowing only for the other person, leading straight to the centre of the earth.

I get called in for a shift. I'm lazy at it and spend the beginning staring at the Filipina waitress who always wears little X-Men bandages to cover up shaving scratches. She's wearing a black skirt that ends before the knees that I think you can see through if the light hits it properly. Always in wedges, lives downtown, and drives her car to work. Melissa tells me that she meant to say pay was coming tomorrow tomorrow not today tomorrow. I cut an apple slice into my mouth. I'm covering for the dessert guy. The Filipina waits for me to plate the cheesecake.

A spray of blood on my coat. Droplets look like they could have come from a small bird's neck, but it's fresh and soaking into my chef's whites. I see a bit of Thomas's thumb where the green onions are kept before I see his face crunched in horror. I catch him in that split second when something awful happens and you've seen it, but you don't know it yet. Then there's a little more blood and Thomas struggling to remain at his station. He's fighting the relief that indulging in something as deep as a scream brings.

That ain't even that big a piece of your thumb. I try to calm him down.

Now he's in the corner in silence, and the sous has noticed and moves the thumb chunk onto a pita and then into a bag of ice. A phone call is made and it's easier to drive him to the hospital than wait for the ambulance.

Sous goes with him and I'm the last one speaking good English tonight, so I stand in front of the line in charge of kitchen staff I barely know. The waiters do their duty to ask if he's okay—only a thumb—and then they remember they have their tips. Water, drinks, quick conversation, and I rally the kitchen.

Tonight I realize how little I know what's going on—what the fuck is Korean food mixed with Italian? I butterfly a chicken breast and ready a pan for it. I stack gnocchi onto a plate, a building of kimchi. The vinegar oozes across the plate to touch the gnocchi. Bala has overcooked the gnocchi, so it's clumping like wet tissue. Bala shouts at me to fuck off, which leaves a silver chain of spit on his face, lip to chin. I could push a knife into him. Such a big chef's knife, seven inches, his soft stomach, the gristle scream of his rib cage. My knowledge of anatomy is useless. I try to imagine what I would cut if I stabbed him from the back, what organs—maybe he would live but his liver punctured, no longer able to drink. I'm stunned at how easy I can picture the knife sliding through his skin to create an open slit, how in my arm I can feel the resistance of his guts, the tug of his insides, the vision of red pouring out over his skin, the rattle of his soulcage, the squeezed whine that would escape from him. I want to apologize to him for the thought, to tell him, Yo, sorry, I'm not usually this goth, but his head is down and he's finishing dishes one by one by one.

The dishes come out looking correct enough. No one can tell, no one complains, and nothing comes back. Bala looks exactly like a pear. His ass dominates his figure, an ass that comes out like the end of the table you always bump into; he constantly interrupts the flow of everyone working. He tells a waitress to fuck off after she compliments us. He's ready to talk about his children at any time.

Why's your face always so screwed up? Janice, the Filipina, introduces herself. Her legs are crossed over one another.

I study her skin and ask her if we're the same shade. She doesn't want to talk to me. I've had three beers. She saves her staff meal for the end of the night and her little goblin mouth. She eats quickly and tells me it's because her father only takes care of her kids 'til twelve. The kids will wake up anyway and search for her, tumbling through the apartment, and cry if they discover their grandfather alone, watching sports highlights.

Janice runs her hands down her legs and squeezes her calves before taking off her wedges. She drops them into a bag. Why are cooks such assholes?

I imagine her as a chocolate milkshake chugging down my throat. You're not supposed to wear nail polish to work, I say with a mouth full of beer.

On the walk home I know I won't sleep. It feels like a cloud is moving through me and slightly untangling my nerves from my brain, so that everything moves slow, good slow, Hype Williams slow, but by the time the sun is cranking over the horizon I'll be exhausted and zombied up. My body is struggling to keep me away from sleep. Sleep feels like it will bring me too close to Anna, so I have to avoid it: What's on that side of the world? Is she waiting there? Could sleep tell me? I know that if you have to sleep, you have to sleep, no one can stop themselves from falling under, but right now, I feel like it's all under my control, that my body is alive and I can manipulate it any way I need. I don't trust what I would see in my dreams.

I remember I breathe, that I control my breath, in and out, in out, that it isn't automatic. I try to stop and manage for about thirty seconds before gasping hard for air like a berserk animal. Was that the last thing I shared with Anna? I remember telling her months ago in Trinity-Bellwoods that I had stopped smoking, but I don't think she believed me because my fingers still stank. I remember the way Abu's hand swung what was maybe the last time he hit me, a low arc, his hand silent near his hip before snapping up into the air, but I was thirteen then and getting quicker, and I was able to pull away before he clapped against the back of my head. His palm hit my ear, turned the lobe inwards, and the pain was slow instead of fast. When I grabbed my ear I could smell him through the wheeze of pain—I could smell all the cigarettes he had pulled from that afternoon, that morning, that day, his whole life, the way that stink gobbled up every corner and carpet of that apartment.

Spadina is quiet. The grocers and shops are shut for the night, but their neon signage breaks through the dark. A few homeless men are tucked into crevices looking for sleep, and the blues bar, Grossman's, only has the tiniest trickle of noise escaping. The roads gleam from the wet of melted snow. The house is empty.

I want to speak to someone, but I don't know what to say. I go onto Reddit and create a username, alqaedagruyere, and go to r/toronto and type up a simple post. It's late now, two a.m., so I don't know if this will get the attention it deserves, but at least it will be up for a little longer than if I did it during the day.

Sharia Law? A Force of Good?
what do all these right wingers want? same thing as all us wahhabis and salafis, right? i think it makes more sense for us to work as 1 unit and reestablish old school rules than do anything new. these men have the same thoughts as us but are too scared to ask for it. why not work with us?

It is too obvious or too late at night. I go to the broader section, r/canada and post:

FUCK ALL Y'ALL
don't think that we're not aware of canada's involvement in the middle east, and that we don't know what to do with you. The toronto 18 were nothing but kids who didn't know what to do and who were sold out by someone pretending to be a brother.

I get a reply almost instantly, someone arguing with me about the logistics of Canada's involvement in the Middle East. I ignore him and google hacksaws, and then post a description of sawing Trudeau's head off. My post has been deleted. I almost stop, my body wants to, but you can't stop thoughts, you can't rise above them: What would it be like instead to tear open Trudeau's throat with my bare hands and enter the wound? Where would that lead? That's too weird for Reddit. Instead:

imagine a line of your premiers and prime minister on their knees in front of that flame and my hacksaw cutting through his neck! isn't that what's being done to our muslim brothers? while we do what? you sell weapons to the saudis while ignoring their destruction and pretending to love us. what does it say in the quran about this?

I stop there. I don't know what it says in the Quran and I'm too worked up to go googling. This energy feels fresh, but I feel dumb. I want to masturbate because some websites say that helps you sleep, and I try to evacuate the anxiety and energy from myself by thinking about Jennifer, but images of Anna come at me easier.

We met during high school at her job at Canadian Tire, where she wore a polo and worked with vacuum cleaners. Her dark hair and skinny bug legs that took over that body. Bernie used to joke with her that she was some sort of horse: all legs. Then she got mad and he would try to explain she was like a beautiful mermaid, but a horse. She asked me out at that location. I think about licking in between her legs, her thighs, and finding the small patch of hair on her lower back, proudly discovering something about her own body for her. It had sprung overnight or something—she said she had never noticed it. I try to stop, but memories start unspooling, us in bed, in a washroom, over a pool table, in bed in bed in bed tangled I sweat and can't cum and fight sadness like blue flame instead. If I let it in, it will burn everything away.

On Reddit no one has responded. I search r/islam for any information about suicide, but I'm inundated by results. Most people seem to think suicides go to hell, because it says so somewhere, but some leave a way out, warning against human judgment, reminding us of Allah's mercy. The posts all turn into squabbles with quotes and YouTube links to internet imams I've never heard of.

Still no response, so I post a new one with a slightly accommodating tone:

> *do you ever think the isis guys are only lonely? like maybe they feel weird and out of place and not connected to things. maybe it's just like a club. like the brown, alienated, disenfranchised boy scouts. you know in syria they have to live like the old ages and they're gonna have to learn how to make a fire and hunt and stuff. it's the boy scouts.*

In about ten minutes a user named cloroxbrwn responds: *You're a dumbass.*

An old friend of mine from high school messages me. Matthew can't handle Hussain—thinks he's too wild, too vicious, too much. He's good for cash, though. Hussain was always scheming back home. We went to high school together for three years before they kicked him out for robbing a kid literally for lunch money. It was dumb to expel someone over five bucks, but also dumb to rob a kid for five bucks, so it was difficult to pick sides. Sometimes me and Matthew will find ourselves back in North York, drunk at some party, and Hussain and other McIntyre kids will be there, and Hussain will be drunk and raging. Last time, there was a fight and he almost bashed someone in with a baseball bat.

The little message beeps and I don't know if I should respond. I'm curious and I need money if Melissa is going to continue being late. My cupboard has a variety pack of Mr. Noodles, three cans of red beans, and a KG bag of rice. I close the Reddit window and look at the message pulsing. I look at my phone for someone to text, but it's late.

We used to do small, stupid stuff together—egg houses, shop-lift. We both spent a month selling weed mixed with oregano before getting our asses kicked. The closest I ever got to getting kicked out was stealing a kid's pager and trying to resell it; I had no real idea how pagers worked. Hussain would run larger operations with the help of an older brother and, eventually, as far as I know, once he got expelled, was taken under his wing. I know he's hobbling along in North York, stringing gigs together.

yo bro

sup man whatre you saying?

not much chillin

yah yah how's your girl

u kno

yah u good? heard about anna

yah man

thats shitty

yah man

she was cool

yah man

that'd be fucked if that happened to me

its ok i guess u going to the funeral

nah dog i got work

where you working now
u kno around
none of that side business eh
lol u kno me always hustling
yah u and ur bro still?
i mean he has his own thing now with textiles
o yah that's punjabi business
yo they got everything covered
what about u
y u need $$$
if theres work u no i don't mind
seen seen
hows the fam
u kno/but for real i can link u up soon
kk
u see this? https://www.youtube.com/watch?v=ztqhrBF0rR8
yo what is that lol
thats hardcore shit
lol thats some isis shit
for real those guys are gs
lol u gonna put me on some watchlist
fuck that man rcmp is dumb they aint no fbi shit
u into that
i dunno my bro sent it its cool
never knew u were that into politics
nah not really but what's right is right u kno
for sure
they gonna come for pakistan next u kno how it is

yah/yo i gtg/lets link up soon
yah for real been too long/u still into sneakers
yah why
kk i got a sneaker thing
o yah? resell?
yah u kno all those fobs at uoft
yo those chinese have mad money
they buy resell tho
for real eh
yah
ok peace man
peace

The sun is coming out violent. One of those days when the rays rip through the cold.

What's in the bag? Matthew ain't happy. He's come by my place with some pizza. I squeeze two slices down my throat and we head out, Matthew giving one last look at the bag on my floor.

Men's Wearhouse clothes.

I was at the mall earlier and saw this old dude put his shopping bag down, and I picked it straight up and ran as fast as I could, mall security trying to smash me on all sides. I ran down the up escalator because I thought it would trick them somehow, but it didn't—of course one of them was waiting at the bottom. He was old; you could see he wasn't prepared for this. He looked Tamil. I went into him with my shoulder, momentum guzzling me past him. Out the door onto Dundas, down Yonge to Queen.

What'd you do with them?

Threw them out. Too small.

Matthew needs extra cash. He's started seeing someone. He doesn't seem to want in on this.

I wanna take her to Montreal. He rolls a blunt and licks it and we gun it down.

You should take her to Jamaica.

Why?

It's hot.

I wanna take her to Montreal for New Year's.

Take her, bro. Like you wanna pay for everything?

Yeah, train, hotel, all that, you know? I want to show her I can. That I got cash for that.

You don't have cash for it.

I want to show her that I do. She ain't looking at my bank account.

You think it's easy to break into a vending machine?

You dumb.

What about that dude that backed his pickup truck into the Loblaws and stole the ATM?

That's stupid too, man, they have cameras. Why you acting like such a waste?

What you mean?

You stole a bag of clothes!

It was thirty dollars' worth.

You got food?

Noodles up there.

What else?

I got an apple around somewhere. It was in that Men's Wearhouse bag.

This is high-school stuff, man. Can't believe you did that.

Pawn a bunch of your shit. Your guitar.

My dad gave me that.

You know how pawnshops work?

Not really. How do they work?

I dunno, man. I think it's like a loan or something.

What if someone buys it?

I don't really know.

The bar is tucked away in an old lane off Bloor Street. We've been coming here since we were nineteen. Matthew has difficulty talking, not talking about himself. Wearing his blue toque crooked, big thin-ass green jacket pinching at his waist too big for his shoulders, he holds his beer with the very tips of his fingers and curls an arm around my shoulders. He puts the beer down and rubs my chest.

You okay?

Fuck, man. Each conversation is like the last one didn't happen: like we rediscover Anna dead all over again. Nah, that's crazy. That's crazy. It's crazy that that happened. Can you believe she did that?

Matthew's come back from a high-school era hangout, sorting out the plans for the viewing with some old friends. The beer tastes like a burlap sack. It moves through me like it owns me. I stop breathing for half a second, for two halves, for three seconds, and Matthew orders another beer. He cancels the order, orders a pitcher—Is that okay?

Yeah yeah yeah.

You going to the viewing?

For Anna? What?

I know, I mean—I just mean. You a'ight?

I need a suit.

I'm too big for you.

I have to see Bernie too. Shit. I haven't seen them in a long time.

Who? Her fam?

Yeah.

They know you broke up?

I don't know. Yeah—Bernie knew when he called.

Did he tell you what she did?

I spoke to him for a minute.

How'd she do it?

I don't know—man, I don't know. I don't know.

He didn't tell you?

He told me that she died. That she killed herself.

You didn't ask—

Why we talking about this?

You don't want to know?

I don't know. I don't know. Does it matter?

I don't know. I don't know if this is true.

What?

I talked to Emina about it. I heard it. She told me.

Who told Emina?

Her family?

Should I get a black suit?

Don't get, like, a tan suit. A grey suit.

Yeah.

Do it up.

I don't have any money.

Go to H&M.

I don't got any money, bro. I got rent. I got some Mr. Noodles money.

I'll bring you a tie. You have a white shirt?

Nah.

You have a white shirt?

I have a white shirt. I have black shoes. Okay.

Easy. Look at this. Matthew shows me his phone. H&M sale on a black suit. The jacket and the pants for eighty bucks.

Who told Em?

I think her family. Do you want to know?

I don't want someone to tell me tomorrow.

You want me to write it down or something? Read it at your own pace?

Nah, man, what the fuck is it?

Pills, she took pills.

For real?

She had a prescription for benzos. I didn't think she would do it that ...

She did.

She was bugging out.

When was the last time you talked to her?

(   )

When?

I don't know.

We slide into a tuck shop on our way home and when Matthew is standing near the cash register paying for a bottle of water, I snatch a chocolate bar into my pocket. I tell him outside while the wind moves shaggy.

For real?

You want some?

What is it?

A Twix.

Nah.

You sure?

You going to go to the mosque?

The mosque? What?

I dunno. To pray.

For what.

For Anna.

Bruh.

I keep imagining Anna in burgundy lingerie, lingerie she never owned, and I flick myself on the nose to get rid of the thought. Little lightning of pain. I can't stop thinking of the way her white skin would have poured through the fabric—I've imagined an intricate one-piece—but I can't bring myself to masturbate to her. I hold my dick, which I do a lot—Anna used to say I was frightened it would disappear—and instead log back on to Reddit. I don't have the energy tonight for theatrics, so instead I post a small thing on sharia law, basically word for word for what I already posted, except this time on the NDP and Conservative Party subreddits. I scan the video Hussain sent me one more time and post it under r/funny, which gets me banned instantly. Finally, I watch the video properly for the first time and it's a little weird, a dumb montage of war scenes, or fighting scenes, and a bunch of blared Arabic. I think they're about to cut some dude's head off, but I close the window before I get to that. That shit ain't gonna help me sleep, and I should be careful about watching stuff on the internet—but if it's on YouTube, it should be okay.

Bernie calls me, wakes me, asks me: Do you need a ride, son?

I hadn't fallen asleep, but I had entered that state of awake-not-awake staring at my wall basically dead but heart beating, and his phone call is super unwelcome. I grumble something at him and manage a basic: nah.

Matthew is coming to get me.

Oh, Matthew, good boy.

First sin of Anna was that she kept me hidden from her family—They're old, you know, this would be weird for them. It would be a thing. Can we not talk about it?

Matthew would go over, though. They had met him at a birthday party, and Bernie and her mom saw that he was dating a brown girl, so he was allowed into the house, past the gates. That was okay.

I'm a little worried about not sleeping. It hasn't happened like this in a while—so many nights wobbling between awake and not. I go onto Reddit again and someone has replied to my post calling me a Paki cunt. Fair enough. I tell them that I'm going to fuck their mom, which is enh, but all I can manage. Someone has replied to my sharia post—

I wouldn't have minded stoning my ex when she cheated on me.

Someone wrote that at 4:56 a.m. I private message him:

sorry to hear that bro

You know, I have to say, I was surprised how many classic ideas of family building were still prevalent in the Middle East. I was there for business, and also in Malaysia, and it was almost all nuclear families.

yeah yo

I mean, obviously, I don't think that high levels of immigration from them are good, and the people are not as tolerant as us, but their economic boom proves that these ideas do work.

what

Instead of having to worry about so many different things, imagine if a core value system was still respected. Women wouldn't cheat because it wouldn't be an idea possible to them, because control would still be in the hands of men.

true i can be scared of women

Well, don't be a pussy. In the Middle East the man is the head of the household and proudly so. It's the pride that we've lost.

is it weird being really attracted to and scared of women at the same time?

I think you guys are lucky: our women are raised to believe ideas of "identity." I still notice that Asians believe in classic modes. Hijabs have got to go though. I love smelling their hair.

sniffing hair is weird

He does not reply to the last message.

I remember all the news shows about fertilizer bombs, and Google brings me to a website pretty quick. This will likely get the most attention on Reddit. A farm fresh ingredient. I like that it's redneck—fertilizer. I'm surprised by how much fertilizer you need for a decent explosion, but whatever, I get a list together and make a series of posts. One on r/canada on how great it would be to bomb Bay Street, one on r/islam asking which is the biggest mosque in Toronto. When was the last time I went to a mosque, twelve? It was a tiny North York one, and even on Eid, it felt barely full. The posts are sincere; I want to know where I can meet the most Muslims. I hope some internet detective will be able to put two and two together, trace the link between my posts that share a username. Could they knock on my door and disappear me to Syria or wherever the fuck and electrocute my balls or pull my nails out? The more tenderness they show when pulling my nails out, the more it will hurt, the slower, the deeper the pain. How does waterboarding work if you know you aren't in water? My body will always betray me.

I don't cut myself shaving. Long, long strokes along the gut of my chin. That girl Jisha liked to watch me shave. Once, she asked me to sit on her sink so she could shave me. She did it way too fast like a maniac, but no nicks, and we went for hamburgers. When we got home I washed my face after eating her out and noticed there were three dark patches of hair on my skin. I got mad at that. I hadn't cum, I wasn't used to a condom after so long with Anna raw, I was tense. She wouldn't see me again: stiff-dick-retard-faggot were her last words on the way out after I had popped off. I still had the condom on, like a porno clown, while I yelled.

I thought I would become an adult when my first friend became pregnant on purpose, but maybe it's now because Anna is dead. No black suit. I didn't buy anything. I manage with grey pants and a white shirt shoved in. I find a tie. The end of it is moth garbled. My hair I've combed to the side, and Matthew's father's Nissan woofs outside on the driveway. I drink my roommate's milk, flatten the box, shove it behind the oven where he won't see unless he's creepy and goes looking. I hear the soft patter of skin from his room: he's fucking his girl. I want to listen, but it almost makes me cry to hear the way her moans curl out into the air and he grunts like some sort of flesh-eating idiot. I wish I had a bazooka.

The Nissan is heated.

Did they have the suit?

No.

Damn. Which one did you go to? The one in the mall?

I didn't go. I got pants. Grey pants. A tie.

It's a funeral.

It's a viewing. What are you wearing? I can't see under his parka.

I got a tie. I got a suit on. Matthew takes off is toque and his head is freshly faded. His skin in the light, light from everywhere: the sun, the snow, I can barely see.

I knew her for so many years.

Me too.

It's not a fucking competition.

Yo. Chill.

Sorry.

Chill. There's gonna be a lot of people there.

Was she popular?

You dumb? How long did you date? Did you talk to her dad?

For a minute.

Since I was sixteen, man.

Matthew lights a twiggy joint. Weed mixed with tobacco, which is okay for driving. A smoke snake slithers out of him and evaporates. He opens the window. I refuse a toke. The viewing is in North York, where her family lives. My sleeplessness is steady: I cannot really keep track of where we're going north of Bloor and into the vacuum of the suburbs. Matthew wiggles the joint in his fingers, puffing smoke in the air, sleep teasing me. I extend my fingers out as far as they can go, open my hands as wide as I can make them, and graze the pebbled contour of the dashboard. It would break my face if we crashed, it's true. My mind flashes to my nose exploding out of the back of my skull like a spaceship and my eyes bulging cartoon like, popping wild and lost on the floor of the car, maybe lost in some grass for a raccoon to eat. How much blood does a human body hold again? Like ten wine bottles?

A loose line in front of the funeral parlour doors and weight gain on high-school friends. Everyone standing around awkward as fuck. I stay in the car while Matthew gets out and greets them. Blue suits, grey suits, pinstripe suits: not a single black one. The sun pours over everything like spilled water, and I'm dying in this car, my skin choking. I knuckle my hands and firm them against the dash.

Bernie and Mary greet everyone. The lump moves inside and I exit the car to follow. I hang back, surprised there's no smokers left. I'm surprised that I don't want a smoke. Inside is warm, like being inside skin. Bernie is alert, firm, flicking the zipper on his sweater that he's wearing under a blazer. He always talks like he's about to confirm the sale of a car—Anna worked for him at his Toyota dealership. He got the dealership late in life, she would say, angry at me for implying wealth. She slapped me once when I called her a rich girl. A small slap, like a joke at first, but halfway through the motion she realized she really wanted to kill me. Mary next to him with the same tight face. They've been together for forty years, I think. They must share skin products; it's like they share skin. It would take a knife to get them apart. No tears, no sobs, only strength. They live in a small little blister of North York that's rich. Anna's brother, Nick, sells weed because he's bored; he knows me the best. I look around for him and he's in the corner, sullen, sober. Next to her parents two pairs of old people I don't recognize, but everything about them is shimmering familiar. They must be grandparents. Matthew shakes their hands. I'm surprised they don't dap, the asshole. Bernie approaches me and blocks me from their view, pulls my hand into his soft paw. It's wet, recently moisturized, and calloused: I know he loves to garden. Anna told me that when she was younger he would spank her with a belt across her ass, never use his bare hand, never hit her on the face. She would talk about the pain with a casualness, like these things were meant to be part of life. She could swallow any sort of grief. So careful the way he shakes hands. A soft grasp, his thumb deliberate on the crease where the index morphs into thumb. He looks at me with his blue saucers, never relenting, daring me to match his stare. His eyes are not empty, but they are not full of what I would expect.

Can we speak after?

Mary smiles; guard-dog teeth protect her guts.

Matthew sneaks ahead of me and visits the body. He pats people on the back and takes on the role of caretaker. When did Matthew become this good at other people? He moves so cleanly through conversations. There are Annas all over the place: fat-cheeked Annas, the serious drawn-out face, the curly hair, seven years old, fourteen years old, thirty years old. Her family is everywhere. The loopy brown rings of hair, the puppy fat on her hips that she boasted about. She would get me to grip it directly when we fucked, or when we hugged; she wanted me to feel her fat—You have a problem with women, you think we are perfect, she would say, and then list off her flaws, like she could be categorized into a series of issues. All the women in the family look the same. I can't tell if my vision is blurry or if I'm going mad. They all look like smudged Anna's. It smells sweet in this parlour, like rot.

This weed is good, yo, if you need to chill.

Where would I smoke it?

I got this vaporizer thing I brought.

Fuck off.

Thin Anna, straight Anna, chubby Anna: like God made her again and again and again and smeared each one different before releasing them out of the cage. The seven-year-old is standing next to me. She looks exactly like her. The thirty-year-old scoops her up and scolds her in a hushed voice. Matthew guides me back into the line to view the body. I can't stop looking at all of them; I want all of them in my life. I want to raise the little one.

It's okay, it's okay, okay? You got this. You got this. You're my dude. Matthew's voice is wet warm in my ear, and I'm happy now that she kept me away from her family. I'm happy there's less to grieve. She was too scared to properly introduce me. That's fine. The sun is here, infiltrating every corner of this room like it has the right to be wherever it wants. It must be the first viewing for so many of us. The first viewing of a friend, of a peer. There are her uni friends, Don Kim wearing olive pants, blending into the green carpet, blending into the plants around the room. Everyone strikes me as impossibly courageous and I am so proud of all of them. Where did they get the energy from? I want this courage to translate in some of these people to mean that they have the instinct to approach me, and maybe they do, but I can only watch, now, the thirty-year-old Anna and the way she holds her child in her arms like she's never going to let her grow up on her. Don is wearing a white T-shirt under his button-up that has the word GHANA splayed across it. He looks tanned. Yeah, rich. I see Bernie peeping my interactions from the corner of his eye, and I swear he almost moves to stop this one:

Son, how do you know her?

I went to school with her.

I'm Anna's grandfather.

Oh.

I've seen her parents seven or eight times only—over ten years! Bernie's away from the rest of her family, at the friend group.

Nick is being a catastrophic weirdo and does not approach me. I see him speaking to Matthew in quick whispers. The weed has mostly worn off Matthew now and he looks sunk. Matthew shrugs his shoulders emphatically at him and Nick moves away. He was asking for weed—Matthew only says no that hard when some kid asks him for free weed. Even the death of a sister wouldn't knock loose enough sympathy in Matthew to part with kush. Nick trawls around the parlour; he's one of those gross little rich white kids who smell like deodorant layered on top of BO, who pockmark basements everywhere with the latest Xbox or whatever, puffs of smoke vanishing upwards towards their parents, who are unsure what to do. I told Anna that her parents should smack him too, and she replied, What, like yours did for you? and that shut me down quick. There's a dude that Nick is talking to, a buzz-cut white dude, Owen, who I know Anna dated for a little. Owen was an official thing for six months not so long ago—two years?—and during a crack in our relationship she posted pictures of the two of them all over the internet, including one that burned me: one with her parents at some picnic in the summertime, the one photo that I don't think I'll ever forget. Owen: what a little goofy-looking dude. I want to slash him, but I wasn't angry, not really. He was good to her. He would have to be—as much as she could destroy herself, she would not permit anyone else to. She was in charge of her destruction. Still, there is an angry new urgency in me that I want to unleash, and the freshness of it is as exhilarating as meeting Anna the first time.

Owen's here with a little blonde and they both look at Nick bug-eyed because the moron is asking them for weed. He thought he could manage the event without a joint, but he probably forgot how long it had been since he had attended a social event without smoke in his lungs.

Matthew's bumbling around—he's taken another quick smoke. Do you think there's food? he asks with clear seriousness.

Do you think this is a party?

On TV there's food.

Emina moves through the crowd towards me. She was a university friend of Anna's. How few people I know here. I can feel so many eyeballs resting on me, but only hers have warmth. She talks to people in short energetic bursts. She's wearing a grey skirt suit combination that broadens out her shoulders. She's tough: went to America for school, played field hockey, but missed Canada too much. Her shoulders are wider than mine and when she hugs me she balls her fingers into fists and the knuckle of her thumb pushes into my back. Is she trying to kill me? She squeezes so hard I see an angel: Jibril and his flaming sword burst into the parlour. No. Is she, though? She could, she squeezes so hard. How many strokes of a hockey stick against my skull would it take to break the bone and smush my brain? One stroke of Jibril's sword is all, I bet. She boxes for fun and hit me once when we drank too much rum, and I choked on the beer I was finishing. When we were younger she had round, sphere cheeks; now they are thinned out a little, serious—she hated looking young. Anna told me that sometimes she missed her period and would run so hard in practice she pissed herself. Emina is one of the few people here who knows the details of my relationship with Anna, who knows the off, on, snap on, snap off nature of it. She could blame me! That is what I am most worried about: who here is giving me stink eye mad vibes because of blame, who lays her death on me for not doing enough. It's slivered up my spine and shut me down; this is why I'm being an unreasonable shit in the corner of the parlour, refusing to talk to anyone. The best friend would have to carry some of the burden too—it would have to be something we shared and used to protect each other. Emina folds her body into mine. Her wet breath on my neck, off, on, off, on, on and on; a little reminder of her soul. She pulls her face away and looks at me, her eyes to my chin, and I stare back, a stuttering fuckhead, until she speaks.

I'm so sorry.

It's okay.

I didn't expect anything—like this. I'm so sorry.

It's cool.

Matthew taking care of you?

Matthew's a good boy. Is Rick here?

He couldn't get off work. He's coming for the funeral. She stuffs her face against me and a grasping sob bucks out of her. Emina pulls away and holds me by the hips, and my hands are on her hips. I take her back into my arms and we pull away again.

Are you coming for the burial?

The funeral?

No—after. There's a ceremony.

She's getting cremated?

There's a burial after—she wanted a cremation; her parents wanted a burial. They're burying some of her, still. Or, the ashes?

I ...

Oh—did Bernie? Matthew knows. Matthew has the details.

They didn't tell me.

Bernie knows about you guys ...

Fuck that old ass.

Omar.

What do you want me to say? Really.

Come. Come with Matthew. He's not going to turn you away.

It's not a dinner. Matthew doesn't get a plus one.

How did Matthew not tell you?

I don't know. I haven't spoken to him about it.

Are you going to come?

I can't force myself in.

Why didn't Bernie invite you?

I don't know him. I don't know them. I don't know who they are. I don't know who he is. I don't know who he is. I don't know her mom. I don't know them. What can I do? I just met the grandfather. I'm not part of this. This is not my thing. They don't know me.

I'm sorry—I mean. Her ashes are going to be buried.

The fuck do you want me to do?

Are you okay?

I'm so good, girl.

Don't.

About what?

About Anna?

I'm not really thinking about it.

That's okay too.

Sure.

Okay.

We done?

Omar.

We done?

Emina is the opposite of Anna. She sees no value in keeping things to herself, and especially not if something meaningful could be reached. Anna was broken off from herself, from me, and I realized it way too late, way too late. It was like she moved with caution, and so she lagged behind everyone a little bit. It meant she saw everything—that her perspective was wide. It seemed natural that I would be protected from the ringing bell of Anna's pain until something like this happened, until she finally made herself public, with a grand, warm cut. When Bernie told me over the phone, it wasn't a surprise. I felt like I have been waiting for this since I met her. It felt quiet, like a known truth finally revealed.

Emina smooths out my jacket and looks at me again. Her eyes are plant green, warm, wet—she doesn't hide them, and apologizes for the small wrinkle on my coat that her fingers can't flatten out. I am tired from being engulfed by her personality and the heat of intimacy that she brings to every exchange. She kisses me on the cheek and tells me she's sorry again. She squeezes my hand, which remains soft, limp; I can't squeeze back.

Sleep sags on me. Matthew has a bottle of Pepsi—where? How? He passes it to me and I pass it back. He swishes it in his mouth. He doesn't realize how stoned he is. He's keeping it together.

Bernie flinging towards me. It's weird how he looks, moving like a bird against the ocean. We're standing near the door and maybe he's worried we're about to leave. Matthew tenses up and raises his hand to his chin and rubs his bare skin.

Matthew disappears when Bernie is in front of me playing with his sweater's zipper. He calls me son. His voice burbles, reluctant to come out. I ask him how he's doing and he flicks his zipper up and down some more, hoping it will reveal something. I stare hard at the YKK notch on it. He asks how I'm holding up. I shrug. Anna said you were a good cook. I shrug again. I'm sorry we never really spoke, he says. It feels like a plastic bag is around my face. I can't really look at him because I start to see Anna in his face, in his forehead. It's hard breathing with him looking at me. He looks at my forehead while I look at the tie knotted at his neck. My first chef used to show me YouTube videos on his phone. He liked to show cook's techniques on it, and he showed me how to skin a chicken once. It was something I never had to do, but he showed me, and now I can't stop imagining Bernie under a glaring light and his bald head being skinned with a Wüsthof.

Do you want to step outside for a smoke?

I don't smoke. Did she leave anything for me?

Bernie clucks. She left some belongings in her apartment—some books. Clothes. I had to move it out, you know. I don't know if anything is yours. Do you inscribe your books?

Hunh?

You know, in school, they teach you to put your name on the inside.

I think I left some clothes with her. She was meant to give me a box.

Of what?

Of things.

I can check. Would it say your name on it? What's in it?

My things.

I knew you were broken up. Recently. I don't think there's a box specifically for you. I can check, I mean. I know it's hard to hear, son, but there's nothing else. I notice Bernie's hands clenching and unclenching in his pocket. He's making a fist over and over again, straining against the fabric of his pants. Why is he doing that? I hear crumpling paper; I see a cleaner in the corner of my eye folding a newspaper. He's waiting to get started on the bathroom. My father used to tell me that all everyone does is lie to you.

There's a note.

There's no note for you.

Bernie—

There's a note for some people. There's not one for you.

What do you mean?

There's nothing with your name on it.

What are you talking about? How could she—

I don't know why she didn't—

Are you fucking serious?

Matthew's in the corner with Em and I can see his eyeballs swerve over to me.

Don't raise your voice, son.

I don't think I raised my voice. How you gonna tell me there's no note?

She left a note for us, for her brother, for Emina, for some others ... She wanted to say sorry. She's sorry.

Are you fucking joking?

Yo, Omar—Matthew is next to me—you got that Pepsi?

Why are you saying this to me?

Omar, I'm sorry. I'm sorry—there's nothing.

Yo Omar, chill, chill, chill chill chill chill chill.

I don't know what noise I'm making. I can't breathe.

Don't say my name.

Matthew puts his hand on my shoulder and squeezes me away. I let him, or am too confused to not. Matthew guides me out down the steps into the cold, then the car.

What kind of person keeps her secrets after death? I thought she would burst open when she died, finally. I stop thinking—I don't want to turn her into thought. I don't want to make her a myth. I don't want to stop being in love with her. Matthew asks me if I want a drink and I wipe the drool from my mouth. I'd spaced out. We're on Yonge now, driving south.

Is there for real not a note for me?

She didn't leave a note for me either.

Dude.

Four years ago we had an apartment together when she first left her parents' place. The apartment near the movie theatre at Eglinton. A squat four-storey building. Eventually, after spending most nights there, I felt pulled towards her and the idea of permanency. My body told me to follow her. Matthew told me not to, but I was confusing gratitude with debt.

I want a note. I deserve one. I don't know what questions it would have in it, but I want something physical of her from beyond. You're dead, really, once you make the decision to die and you begin those notes. Anytime I had thought about dying myself, it was the note-writing that always stopped me. Putting in ink the thoughts that moved around in me was too much. I wanted pleasure only, not to confront my own viciousness, or even Anna's. Those pleasures that I always had access to with her—the tactile, her body, food, her laugh—I knew I would have to keep her away from my darkness to preserve them. I wanted too many shallow, pleasant insights, and quick, repetitive happiness; I did not want to risk discovery. I did not have the endurance for something deeper.

I feel like a canvas stretched out a little too long. There's a wrongness in my vision, as if everything has been coloured fucked. Cities should be built in pink and blue candy colours to keep us interested. That would be the best way to kill myself, riding over the skyline in a hot air balloon, looking down on the city, the streets like fingers extending from a hand trying to escape itself.

I wonder if she was thinking about the first time we touched—both our hands reaching for the bill, our knuckles clacking—and if it was in the note. I wonder if I ever told her I shaved for the first time that night, put on too much of my father's aftershave, without smelling it first, and then washed it off. I didn't know what to do with my hair, but I bought product and slicked it loosely back. I practised two nights in a row after my evening shower. I wonder if she noticed me staring staring staring trying to memorize every tiny detail of the evening because even though I'd seen those other girls, I'd never been on a proper date, but it felt right to take her out to dinner. I had been told about love my whole life but didn't realize how greedy I was for it, didn't know how a small sliver could explode me. I wonder if she knew the moment that I fell in love with her was a tiny sentence, and I can see now the trap that a small gesture could hold me so powerfully.

I still can't sleep. Matthew is on the couch in the living room. From my open bedroom door I can see him watching *Rumble in the Bronx*. I'm watching the sun move up through the kitchen window, stoned out of my gizzard, sleepy as the heat pulls over my body. In the middle of a toke and I remember roommate does not like when I smoke inside, but I'm on the lease so fuck him. I push out the smoke like gunshots. Roommate is in his underwear preparing two bowls of cereal with a delirious delicacy. He drops berries into the bowl. They are new: they fuck a lot. He smells like sweat.

You kinda smell like pussy, I say. It's the kind of joke I think he might like, but he says, Oh, quietly, and stops with the cereal. He takes the bowls inside his room and leaves the raspberries on the counter. I crush them in the plastic box and lick the juice off my fingers. I'm trying to figure out if the light changes as it comes through the windowpane. I do this by chucking my head up and down, alternating between the window and real life, faster and faster, until it's impossible for my brain to tell if I'm looking into open air or through glass.

I've spent the night on Reddit and their amateur porn r/gonewild section where women (mostly) post photographs of themselves. I found myself recently drawn to testicles, the way they slacken and loosen or tighten when a body is moving furiously (Google says they retract to protect themselves), and I'm always too high to tell if the fascination is sexual or only weird. Some of these photographs are filter fake, but most of them startle me in their realness, and each photograph, or collection of photographs, is followed by comments. Most photographs are poorly themed and choreographed—quick snapshots in mirrors. Some have been shot using a tripod (you can see the woman holding a remote shutter release), and some have a male partner, a dick suddenly bursting into a scene near the end of the series.

Ninety-eight percent of the photographs are bodies: The heads cut off by the frame, blurred using Photoshop, or with an emoji pasted over them. The bodies are white, generally, unless they are Asian. Sometimes black or brown. You have to search hard for black or brown, and not hard for Asian. The Asians always tell you they are Asian.

In the search field I type Anna's height, 5'4", which doesn't get anything, really, so I type in *brunette*, which gets too much. I try different words—*pale, short, brown hair*, click click click, and I find a girl who's shorter and chubbier but otherwise close. She has no face and has been posting for two years and has about fifty photographs of her naked, headless body.

Now, in the morning, in front of the bedroom window, I feel a switch of regret come on. The sun looks like a crescent moon through the glass, covered a little by the clouds and pollution, snowflakes dropping onto the city. A small Chinese-looking woman is jingling through the recycling and she takes out a wine bottle. I wish I could give up on breathing. It's unfortunate you can't turn your lungs off like that. It's not like opening and closing your fist, or your legs.

There were gangly pimples on Alex, the last woman I slept with. They were on her back and her shoulder, a crazy gang of red lumps. When I was behind her I put my hand on them and clutched her flesh and muscle, and she screamed because the pimples were raw. She squirmed off my dick and we had to stop momentarily because the pain was sharp.

Anna didn't have flawless skin, but not skin like that, not skin that caused her pain. She had white flesh that went red when she came.

Lunch shift is full of new white people: a grungy greased face, and a blond with black streaks. The eggs are reminding me a little of wombs. The squiggly yellow eye in the middle. This is a short shift that I'm covering for someone and I've never cooked this many eggs in a row. I make small mistakes, bump into things, forget that I'm stoned-ish. Is exhaustion one of those features of life that you get used to? Like sadness and disappointment? Or is it more of the body: hunger or thirst, that I'll die if I'm exhausted? I sip my coffee and look at Melissa. I try to make her remind me of Anna. The way she walks does a little, but I'm making that up.

When Alex pulled away from me she told me something so simple:

That hurt.

I'm sorry.

It's okay. Let's not do it like that. Come here.

Can I be really weird with you?

What do you mean?

Can I be really, really weird?

What?

She was laughing and apprehensive at the same time. My dick was hard in the rubber, saluting straight at her.

Never mind.

No! Tell me!

No, never mind, it's fucking weird. Put me in.

Do you want me to speak Chinese?

What—!

It's okay, guys have asked me that.

Really? Oh, okay.

No! Jesus!

I lay flat against her and tucked my face into the pillow. I had, for a second, wanted to ask if I could tell her I loved her, for fun, to relax, but I got hold of my craziness.

Melissa makes eye contact with me whenever she pops into the kitchen, and I drink a bunch of coffee. This job is $11.50 an hour—what do I need the money for? I don't know—so I can launch myself to the moon. Maybe I'll go to Cambodia and eat spoonfuls of noodles until I'm deranged. She's beautiful and I think about spitting blood in her mouth. I land two perfect sunny eggs onto a plate.

Right after we broke up, Matthew was really hyper about me getting laid: You need to fuck, you need to fuck someone, seriously, man, how are you going to get over her? This was the most basic advice and I had done it and tried to do it—to get over her. I allowed myself into bars, but too many drinks erased me, over and over again. I don't know how I struck with Alex, except that I knew her a little from before and that worked in my favour. The next time I went out with Matthew to get laid, we got kicked out of El Mocambo because I lit a small flyer on fire over a flaccid table candle.

When I think of fucking, nothing is normal—a fantasy of Melissa, interrupting me eating her out to tell me that her period has started; a coil of shit turtling out of a black girl squatting; a clump of red hair coming loose in my palm as she goes down on me; vomit on my cock. The lights too dark, the lights too dark, the lights too bright. The horror of not knowing what to do with a new body, and she must be different from Anna in a million ways but also essentially the same, with legs and breath and a heart like an electric shock. The duplex of fingers Anna liked in her pussy and ass and the way it made her cum; would that trick work on someone else?

Lunch finishes and I wrap a steak in my apron to take home, hoping the meat will put me to sleep later. I scroll through my phone, looking for someone to text something relaxed to, to calm myself, but I don't know if behaviour comes before feeling or feeling comes first. I feel like eating a chainsaw, so I put my phone away.

Grappa's has a one-day-only menu that Melissa tells me to forget—These are my recipes! and she's only half joking. Everyone in this kitchen is insecure except for Sachiv. I drag an anchor around during dinner rush and fuck up way more than I should. Melissa, angrier and angrier, this new vein popping in her forehead. Her beautiful Helvetica menu goes to waste as hairs loosen from her tight bob.

Omar, what the fuck are you doing?

This simple refrain takes me away from Anna. I plate twenty perfect dishes. I take a rag and wet it, bundle it in a tight roll and wipe the edges of each plate clean. Everything becomes perfect. Melissa loosens up.

Diners come here from Rosedale. I think; I don't know. I've never been to Rosedale. One of the waiters tells me this. I have a small piece of orange cheesecake on the side that I take spoon after spoon of. I haven't eaten since last night's steak; my stomach feels permanently clenched. A waiter drops a plate on the ground and the pieces fly. He fights with Sachiv about cleaning it up. A thick piece of veal is bleeding on the ground. The waiter pulls one of the brown busboys and gets him to clean the mess. Being brown in the front of house means that Melissa doesn't want you to talk to anyone. Melissa fumes and fidgets because they're standing still for the first time tonight; she's scared someone might speak to them and unleash their Bengali English.

He's the kinda guy that calls curry sauce, Harley says. He strokes his dreadlocks.

Matthew has found a table with his girl, Sylvia. He finds me, his head suddenly in the kitchen. Wagwan, yo. Nice dreads.

Harley fingers his locks, unsure if he's been complimented. He looks at Matthew's ripe flesh. Matthew forgets how dangerous he seems—brown and muscular, his smile a slash.

You done soon?

Ten minutes.

That's Sylvia. Matthew points. She notices. She's fine, yeah?

How old is she?

Twenty-five.

She looks young.

Black don't crack, Harley says. He fingers his dreads some more, aching for a way into our conversation. Matthew looks at him until he leaves our space.

Come chill when you're done, Matthew says.

A'ight, gimmie ten. I wipe my knife on the front of my pants.

It's Bala's turn to close. I squirt some cleaner over my station and give it a quick wipe. Melissa is late with the pay again, and Harley keeps telling me how he'd cut her hands off and sell the manicure. Harley is furious and contained. I want to slap him. Melissa's right foot escapes her stiletto and she scratches her calf—I can feel a phantom movement in my own calf, the bristle of her right big toenail against me. She holds hands with the older male customers. She takes both of their hands in hers and talks to them with an open face. She's so good at it their wives don't mind. She paid Sachiv. I tell Harley this and he won't complain—he won't walk off the job. The dishwasher always gets paid on time.

I couldn't see from the kitchen, but Matthew has brought me a surprise—this girl Kali. I had mentioned her to Matthew, and we creeped her on Facebook together, discovering that she was Sylvia's friend. Kali's a short-haired Hare Krishna, and I don't know exactly how I know her. I think we met through a mutual friend at a concert, and then we would exchange hellos, head nods whenever we saw each other at an event or a party. I always remembered the tautness with which she carried herself, her assuredness, and when I saw her at a basement party two months ago, drunk and fiddling with the aux, we talked blackout talk for about twenty minutes before making out in a corner.

I smell like oil sugar sweat. I smell candied. We order drinks. Kali is wearing heels with a floral skirt and a black top; Sylvia is the opposite. They joke about this—Sylvia's shirt is floral, her skirt is black, her skin is black too, where Kali is white and purple and red with embarrassment when me and Matthew mention she is the sole white one at the table and we are the only dark customers.

I begin speaking to Sylvia, like I'm giving a speech: my name, what I do, where I live. I pretend I live in a condo and Matthew's eyes bug out. I focus on Sylvia because Matthew has brought her here to meet me and I want to do something well, to meet her well. She looks me in the eyes too much. She wags one leg over the other, her thighs touching, her calves in the open air, a small bit of her thighskin stuck to the vinyl of the seat. I realize she wouldn't know who Anna is! Would Matthew have told her? Would he have interjected that grief into a beginning relationship—no. Wouldn't it be better if I made Anna up? There is a lightbulb above us attached to a long cord and it swings back and forth like a body. Sylvia's laugh carries her neck back as her hands rise.

I've bottomed four drinks now. I forget the rest of her answers, the question; my hand is on Kali's thigh. I remember she's been working for a catering company and she tells me she's looking for a real-person job. I embellish my lie and tell her the condo is in the financial district. Isn't that expensive, she asks. Yes, I say, and we are joking along—Matthew bug-eyed, still, no one sure who is lying or joking or being mean. I tell Kali it's okay, the condo has a big window and a pool. The drink leaps into my blood. The light moulds into the paint on the wall, and I sway, or the room sways, back and forth, like a building asleep and murmuring. Lights are ghosts, you know, they are electricity's ghosts. I see a turquoise bra peeking from near Kali's armpit.

Rain is foaming outside, so they go home in a taxi. I kiss Kali on the cheek and look Matthew in the eyeballs and tell him Sylvia's a good girl. Matthew asks me what time I work tomorrow and I tell him to mind his own business and slip on the curb. I don't realize it's ended. My teeth gnash into each other and on the way home I see a For Sale sign stuck in a lawn and pull it out and shove it into the soft soil of the flowerbed in front of my house. I hope our house will be sold by morning.

How much has technology aided suicide? There's a bunch of boys in South Korea who have died from playing *StarCraft* too long. They forget to eat, drink ... Do they shit themselves? Some wear diapers. I wish I was that dedicated to anything! Do they ignore the shit because of the press of combat? I regret now not being into video games and the lunatic community they provide of yelling and screeching over headsets, strolling through the internet to find the perfect combat keyboard and mouse, logging in and having instant connections with Chinese and Russian and Arab kids. The perfect flickering friendship designated by code names, signing on and off, killing. Bridges, even, in human history, are new. These high bridges that carve the sky over water and roads: technology to jump off. New-age suicide by Kool-Aid. The range of Japanese vending machines: dildos, panties, cigarettes; I could have taken Anna there for vacation and chosen a suicide machine: a one-time-use gizmo that squishes a knife into your abdomen.

I call Hussain and arrange a meeting with him. He says he has spent the week in jail over some dumb internet shit, but we are still on. Our whole lives he has never tired of doing dumb-ass shit and I don't bother to ask what it is this time. He wants me up in North York tomorrow. I won't tell Matthew because he doesn't understand the appeal of nullifying stupidity.

Matthew is meant to come over, so before he does I log on to Reddit. The r/toronto and r/canada subreddits are quiet. I can feel the lack of sleep pulling me down. I need a quick one:

> *a really simple scenario. bay st. uhaul truck. fertilizer and rye. and like some ghetto home hardware alarm clock bomb thing. all the hot dog stands at lunch hour and all the pink, suited bay street dudes. what's that big bank downtown? i think i could probably drive up the stairs and go right thru the glass windows. although then i guess i'd be blown up too. ok, i could park it close to a building. like really close so the distance wouldn't matter and maybe there'd be enough street traffic.*

Are you angry at her? Matthew looks away when he asks.

For what?

For killing herself?

What do you want?

It makes me angry.

What doesn't?

For real.

What do you have to be angry about? What'd she do to you?

Come on, yo. Don't act like I ain't involved.

You're not involved.

Bro.

Did she leave you a note?

What note?

I don't know. Saying something.

Hunh?

What you mean, hunh? Did she leave you a note?

Nah, man.

(   )

Nah! She didn't. She didn't leave me nothing.

Is Matthew lying—no, he wouldn't. He couldn't.

I can't eat around him. His elbows on my kitchen table and his fork in his closed fist and he scoops the pasta I made for him. He scrambles Nathan's pine nuts over it and parmesan cheese. The tunnel of his neck bulges because he doesn't chew properly. He inhales water. I see the way his hands move when he tells a story. He uses them to frame his argument. He holds the story, cupping and curling his fingers through empty space.

Sylvia calls while we're smoking one, and we fall out the front door together and head to the bar. The light comes on and off our skin, moving with the candle at our table, the flame bickering with the air, waiters at the front door, gently urging us out, as it's past midnight.

Yo, do me a favour.

Anything. Matthew puts Sylvia's hand in his.

Don't tell Kali about Anna.

Yo ...

Nah, don't, man.

Why?

Because.

Because why, man? That's weird.

It's not weird. I don't want her to know.

Do you like her?

I want to call her.

Yo, that's weird. Matthew looks at Sylvia. Sylvia's the one who has to keep quiet—Matthew has to convince her to keep quiet.

It's my business.

It's my business.

It's more my business.

I knew her as long as you did.

Why you acting like you had a separate friendship?

We did have a separate friendship!

You knew her through me.

I knew her for ten years too.

Through me!

So?

So? So she's mine and you knew her through me. It's my relationship.

Bro, I was friends with her. Anna was my friend.

So what the fuck does Kali need to know about it for?

She doesn't, but you can't tell me who to tell.

Don't tell Kali. Do me a favour.

Homie, nah. Why don't you want her to know?

Because it's none of her business.

What if Sylvia told her?

Did you tell her?

Nah, nah—you don't have to answer that. Matthew does not let her answer. You're being fucking weird.

This whole bar is blue, which is a bad colour for a bar. It makes everything feel wet. I feel zonked. Sylvia smiles and her teeth are thick and I sink into a memory of Anna's braces, but I scatter it and focus on Sylvia's collarbone. We get up to leave. I stumble against a chair on the way out. Matthew is carrying a small canister of Tiger Balm and he gives me some to put on my temples and I dab it straight under my nose, which makes me cry a bit.

What you want me to say, man?

I don't want you to say anything—it's a little weird. Why should everyone know what's going on in my life?

If you like this girl, maybe she needs to know that your ex, you know, died. Recently.

She doesn't need to know anything about me.

You like her or you just wanna fuck her?

I've known her for how long? It's a friendship. We been texting.

You know her from before.

She cute.

I can't not tell her this.

It's weird for you to tell her.

How?

To open up to her.

How is that weird?

You don't know her.

Sylvia knows her.

Did she tell her?

Nah! Nah, don't drag her into this.

I don't understand why you have to tell her anything about me.

I'm not telling her anything about *you*.

You're being fucked up about this. Matthew pulls Sylvia to the side and apologizes. He's gotta take care of me, I hear him mumble. He tucks Sylvia into a taxi.

How come we never see birds in the winter? Where all the fucking seagulls at?

They fly to Florida.

Seagulls?

Yeah.

Nah, man.

Bro.

Nah.

What else they gonna do? It's too cold out here.

Remember when Hussain nailed that seagull with the rock.

That guy was a moron.

He's helping me out.

With what?

Some money shit.

The rock hit the seagull in the throat and tore open the flesh. Before it died, Hussain picked it up and held it upside down by its feet; its blood ran over its beak and head, turning its white feathers red. He pretended to take a bite and then flung it into the sandpit in the park.

That boy was wild.

That's psycho shit.

Remember you and him, though?

Selling oregano to dumb-asses? He made enough money. We didn't work for a bit.

So why you gonna get caught up with him now?

He wants to sell shoes or something.

To who?

I dunno. I think he's got some fakes.

You gonna walk down the street selling shoes?

I dunno. There's gotta be some cash. You wanna help?

Nah.

Nah?

Nah, why ... why would I want anything to do with this?

I dunno.

This is dumb.

You gonna get me money?

How much do you need?

I don't want you to lend me money.

I don't wanna lend you money either, man. I'm asking.

Don't worry about it.

Yo, don't do anything with this guy.

Yo, don't tell Kali.

Honestly, I already told Sylvia.

So?

So? She's tight enough with Kali, she would have told her.

I don't think so—she wouldn't have agreed to see me that night.

Why?

Because that's fucked up. Why would you wanna hang out with someone whose ex killed themselves?

She seems nice. She's a Hare Krishna, or whatever the fuck.

That's crazy too.

They're nice.

Nah, man, they're weird. That shit is weird.

Chill.

That's some white people Hindu nonsense. That shit is weird.

They're peaceful.

And weird.

Your boy Hussain kills birds.

We were kids.

We were teens.

Whatever, man. Don't tell Kali.

You creepy ass.

Hussain gets me to meet him at Fairview Mall. Growing up, this sprawling enterprise was a little ghetto full of Persians and too much cologne; now it's Chinese people and high-end stores. I pop out at Don Mills station and wander through the parking lot. He's near the doors, smoking, wearing a big brown bomber. His hair is tight and high, and he has three overlapping gold chains on. He looks the same as when I last saw him two years ago.

What's good? he says, and ashes. He smokes with his index and thumb on the cigarette. The wind curls around everything. We dap and he gets right into it.

You ready?

For what?

We gonna do work.

Oookay.

This is gonna be easy. I talked to this kid on Craigslist and he's bringing three pairs of Yeezy 2s.

Cool. How much?

I dunno. Doesn't matter.

Why not?

'Cause we gonna take them, you dumb fuck.

Uhhh ...

Uh, what?

We loop around the parking lot and behind the subway station. There's a small building, a little farther away from cars, with no security cameras visible. I stand still, unsure what to even begin to do. I seem frozen in time—but that's a lie. I don't want to participate in this, but I want to watch it happen. This poor kid. A Porsche Cayenne goes over a speed bump a little too fast and parks near us. One single Korean-looking kid gets out and gazes at us. Hussain greets him. He pops his trunk open and Hussain walks over while I stay a little bit back. Hussain is moving swiftly and the kid is a bundle of nervous energy. He doesn't speak much English. He didn't bring anyone with him? We're a little deeper into the parking lot now; it's one of those halfway-underground ones. I peek around: no security guards. No people. The wind goes right through me. Hussain inspects a box. He looks at all three. Why is he drawing this out? Hussain stacks the boxes on top of each other and says, A'ight, man, thank you, and pats the kid on the shoulder twice, hard, a third time, super hard. Kid has an undercut and glasses and Adidas track pants on. He is obviously rich, obviously rich and into not looking rich, but even his track pants are the nice ones. Watching this happen in front of me is a little like seeing blood pour out of your own skin from the smallest of cuts. Or is it like when you cut yourself and you don't feel pain until you see blood or your girlfriend tells you that you should be in pain. The kid says something and Hussain says, What? What? and looks at me and says, Let's go. The kid is frozen. He watches Hussain and he sees me and I think notices that I am not capable of doing any violence, maybe letting it happen, and says he is going to call the cops and Hussain gives me the boxes to hold and does something to the kid—I dunno what, but the kid cowers, he moves back and is now sitting in his SUV somehow and shaking and trembling, and this is going on way too long, but the weirdest bit is how slow we are walking away.

Three pairs! Hussain is jubilant, and he throws me a box. You a size ten? Whatever, sell that shit on eBay.

I enter the subway and put my token in and drop downwards past the first and second levels towards home. My hands are warm. In the cove of the train, I feel my mind quieten and melt into my body for the first time since Bernie called. I'm scared; I know it will only last until I have to exit and walk home, and I won't be able to coax it back.

My mind's silence is rare. My high school had a sliver of a stream, and in between spit contests and pot tokes, I sat next to it, listening to water make its centuries-old course. Even with the burble of nearby traffic I could hear this quiet. The noise was soft and made mostly when water was impeded: by rocks, branches, garbage. It bubbled when it broke, noise and form escaping at once. That was enough. A sense of real would cloud me and soothe the anxiety that chattered in my brain. I didn't have to think of home or class, and I could pretend that this peace was real life. The refuge lasted five, ten minutes, until the bell rang, or someone found me, and I was brought back.

Outside Spadina station the sun is pushing rays over everything. I can barely see. I walk slow and I swear there is this black bust-up Honda following me, like a smear. I feel like I've seen it everywhere at the periphery of my vision. I walk down Baldwin Street and pause in front of my place, and it turns left to follow me. Maybe they don't care if I know. I enter my house and go upstairs.

A knock.

Two knocks.

I come downstairs and open the door. Two guys, one brown, one white, both thick shit, like made of wood; white dude maybe more lumpy, at least a gut that's trying desperate to peek from in between his buttons.

Omar? Brown guy speaks my name with familiarity.

I don't recognize him, or his voice, but it's hard and directed straight at me. Their whip is parked in my driveway and I take a look from the door. It's the Honda.

Who're you?

I'm Detective Constable Kevin Mohammad. He doesn't extend his hand or show me ID.

So?

This is Detective Constable Ryan Prescott.

Prescott is standing slightly behind Mohammad, with Mohammad's shoulder eclipsing his body. Prescott offers me a tight lip movement—something like a smile. They look like TV cops, even. Their faces are pulled tight across their skulls, and for a second, I swear their skin is transparent. I notice too—my body, tight in the door frame, my heart pushing faster, sweat on my palms, and the maw of my chest closing.

Okay.

Can we come in?

No.

It's a little cold outside.

Get a coat.

Is this how you want to start this?

Start—

Omar—

What?

We want to talk to you about Hussain.

Who's that?

Hussain Syed.

That's a popular name. I say this while my heart opens in me. There's a hand in my chest now, ripping through all my organs and guts. Are these guys cops for real? Do you have ID? They show me badges.

Can we come in now?

I don't know Hussain Syed.

I mean the one you were with at Fairview Mall. You know where that is?

How rich was that fucking Asian kid? How did their car follow me? How long have I been seeing them from the corner of my eye? Right now, the way my heart is pounding, it feels like my whole life.

When?

Just now. The detective smiles wide. He has a gold tooth hiding in the back. Prescott hasn't said a word.

No.

No, you still don't know him?

No, I don't know you.

Omar—it's okay. We're not here for that. That was small-time. Shoes? Who gives a shit?

Do I need to have this conversation? My voice stays mostly flat while I say that. My blood! I had looked around the parking lot. No one saw us. Hussain was the professional. Do you have a warrant?

Calm down, buddy. There's lots of time for us to work through this.

I try to remember the last time I posted on Reddit and how exactly, I mean, in what way exactly, I talked about blowing something up.

I don't need to be about this.

Come on, now. He extends a hand with a card dangling. I leave it hanging. We're introducing ourselves. I think it'll be good to get to know—

Nah. I'm too terrified to keep speaking, and I shut the door and clench and unclench my hands and do like the internet says and count to ten: one, two, three, four, five, six, seven, and I don't think I turn and open the door and—vanished.

I don't have much of anything left in me tonight, but I manage a post on Reddit:

> *i can't believe canadians are so whatever about what we're doing in afghanistan and the middle east. it proves that canadians are all talk. we're gonna chop their heads off here in toronto, forget what is happening over there. they bring the war to us over there but they forget we're here too. what are the cops gonna do? you know how easy it is to fill up a uhaul with whatever and park it outside a big building. how many uhauls are in the city in downtown at any time? they spend millions of dollars every year on these dumb ass cops and still they can't stop anything.*

I spend the next days on Reddit, posting, deleting, reading, researching. I don't remember the last time I went out, and I order the cheapest pizza special I can find online.

Matthew rings me worried. I tell him I'm fine. He asks me to come see him and Sylvia, to go out and have a nice time. He bribes me with the promise of Kali. I tell him I can't afford to eat and he tells me not to worry.

I meet them at a small restaurant and criticize the bits of the kitchen I can see into—who knows why. Sylvia has on a deep vermilion lipstick that flushes against her skin. Matthew is wearing a navy sweater. Who knows what I'm wearing. I showered before

I came and I can smell Nathan's Old Spice body wash on me. There is a hesitance to me, to the night, but we move swiftly into a taxi and Sylvia asking me many questions and me yammering in careful crescendos, crafting an oral history without Anna. I think Sylvia has a lazy eye; sometimes it seems as if she's looking at everything but me.

We meet Kali at a small barely lit bar on Dundas. I cup Kali's ass, everyone already faded by the time we reach, and she twists her neck to kiss me. She stops kissing me and tells me her tongue might taste weird because of new medication she's on. It tastes like metal, like I'm being poisoned, but I swipe at her anyway. My hand reaches past her skirt and into her panties, but she stops me and moves towards the bathroom, tugging Sylvia with her. Me and Matthew retreat to the bar, my dick enraged, engorged; I realize he'll be the same.

I don't remember the rest, but with my dick hard and my nimble mind drunk, trying to text her now, I don't think I got laid. Matthew is not on my couch, so he went home with his girlfriend, his partner, Sylvia. Nathan is fucking his new girlfriend: I hear nothing for five minutes then a soft moan and nothing and fast pumps of skin on skin and then a terrifying grunt and if I listen closely I can hear the bed shift, tangential laps of his tongue and her small orgasm.

I'm convinced Kali has not heard of Anna. We've moved to somewhere at College and Bathurst and she's hovering under a fluorescent light while a firefly-looking joint buzzes between us. We're at the side door, outside. I'm with Matthew and his friends—three white guys. I refuse a toke; most of me feels like it's ready to vomit. There's a gurgling nonchalance in my gut that I've gotten used to. Her laugh pops from the back of her throat and lurches into the air. The street light is a spotlight on her and her jacket is zipped halfway up. While dancing, the gin and tonics loosen me up (I've had three), and I can feel the jiggle of her limbs. I move my neck low to kiss her and she keeps her lips pursed but moves her ass farther into me so that it feels like her whole body is swallowing me up. She turns around and moves her mouth towards mine for a kiss. It feels like when a wave breaks on shore. We relax. My tongue parts her lips; there is no taste, or maybe that metallic zing again. She punches her tongue out, a belt being snapped. I want that flabbiness of her tongue to collapse softly against mine, not to move sharply like it is. I grab a chunk of her ass into my hands. Lights up: it's 2:30 a.m.

You going home? Kali asks.

I think with Matthew.

Where is he?

There?

Are you hungry?

We pour out of the place.

Did you find Matthew?

No.

I have to get up early for yoga.

Down Spadina the taxi had let us off at the wrong place, so we're walking towards Dundas and her apartment (a unit shaped from the third floor of a house), but first we stop in a Viet restaurant lit up so bright it's daytime and it sobers me up. It's open twenty-four hours. She orders for us and I am staggering around and Kali sits next to me and I have not said much except to tell her that's weird, her next to me, but she doesn't move.

Did you and Matthew have a fight?

Tonight?

Sylvia said you guys had a fight?

No. Tonight?

About Anna?

Who's Anna?

Oh, Omar, I'm sorry—

Why would I want to talk about Anna with you?

I'm sorry! I'm sorry.

She takes both of her hands, which are small, and cups my face and turns my head and kisses me. It is not good to make a person feel bad, Anna once said, or maybe my father, but it is a good way to get things out of them. Whenever whoever said that, I thought of that magician's trick of pulling handkerchief after handkerchief out of someone's throat.

Food arrives one hot dish after another and the restaurant chubbies up as clubbers get inside and there's a small fight between a couple and the one friend is next to them cackling, but he's the girl's friend. The boy hits him right in the face. The two boys fight—a gold chain, fake gold, rips off and flings right next to me and I fight the urge to scoop it up. Kali is calm throughout the whole thing.

That's a nice chain.

Oh my God, don't take it.

Should I take it?

Don't take it! Don't get us involved.

Sometimes drunk bravado is funny, and I try to measure if this is that. She is tense with the violence coming near us. The fight stops. They leave. The chain is taken by one of them.

Are you from here?

Sure.

Omar.

From North York.

Did you know I'm American?

Sure.

We came here when I was five. I'm an immigrant.

You're white.

I'm an immigrant, still.

Did you take ESL?

I mean, I'm white.

You have a beautiful smile.

When I was a kid we lived on this farm for a year and we had four gerbils, Frank, Hank, Ronnie, and Murphy, and I was like eight, and I loved them, I loved them so much. My parents had decided that month that we were going to try and eat meat—at least, meat that we could catch or hunt or gut and dress ourselves. They were still Krishnas, but they wanted to blend it with something. I don't know. My parents spent a lot of time doing that sort of thing. Anyway, we didn't have that many visitors, so when we did, that rare occasion, it was a big deal, like a big, big deal. My mom used to work in a restaurant—did I tell you that?

No.

She did, she was a chef, mostly French food, I think. She used to make dope sauces. So this family came down from when we lived in Newark—did I tell you that?

No.

There's a lot of Indians where we used to live. I was playing with these gerbils and then they came over—the Allisters? I can't remember. Something like that. Something white! And they came over and I left the gerbils out of their cage, but I clearly remember closing the bedroom door. I remember that—isn't that so weird? I remember shutting the door, I remember the click, it was a tricky door, and I know I closed it because I remember that it clicked, and it was one of those doors that had to click to close, otherwise it would swing open with the wind or whatever. So I closed it. I played with this kid, this boy, Tom. I had gotten a bike and my dad bought a second bike too, like a really shitty one, for whenever we had guests and they had kids. There was a little pond and we went to hang out at the pond. And then guess what!

The gerbils were gone.

The fucking gerbils were gone! All four! And you know what else I remember that night?

Is this like a weird first kiss story?

No! Omar! No! I was crying and crying and crying, and my parents didn't even care! And that little kid Tom was like, Gerbils don't live long anyway, I have a dog, that stupid piece of shit. And then we had soup! Some Peruvian soup—

You remember that it was Peruvian?

My dad spent some time in Peru. And it was a fucking meat soup! And my parents wouldn't say what it was! They ate my gerbils!

When the noodles are finished, she drinks her broth. It trickles down her chin. The dumplings are cool on my tongue. Kali watches me slurp them up. She asks me if I know any after-hours and I do not, but she has beer at home, and we finally head that way.

Kali's knees are red and she pulls off the socks she has on. They reach all the way to her thighs. Her knees are red like blisters. There's a series of Balinese masks hanging behind her, above her desk, that I thought were African; she got them after she spent a few months backpacking in Asia. She's wearing a rugby shirt, and when she takes it off, she has on a purple bra and purple panties, but they aren't the same purple. The panties are lace and her bush peeks out a little from the top; the bush is wild, but her legs are smooth. Her asshole is hairless and tasteless and she squirms herself into my face when I lick at her and I believe this has to be God-given. She jerks me off a bit too hard.

They're Hare Krishna's.

Does that mean you're vegetarian?

I'm not Hare Krishna.

Are all Hare Krishnas white?

I mean, I was. We left. I left. They've been Hare Krishna so long I think it's impossible, you know, for them to leave. Like they remember all the old stuff. It's part of them. They just act Hare Krishna.

I think you're always, like, your religion, you know? No matter what. Like the axis is always that religion.

The pole, she says.

Krishnas seem like nice people. Hella calm. Do you ever go to that big-ass Hare Krishna festival on the Island?

Is that Hare Krishna?

There's a lot of white people with shaved heads.

Oh. Do you hate white people?

Yes.

Omar! Don't joke. Do you want to hear about it? There's more to it than that. I'm not in it anymore.

Do your parents live on a farm still?

They do. In Woodstock. In New York? It'll be nice when I'm old.

Do you get the farm?

I think that's the plan.

What if your dad has gambling debts?

I bet your dad is addicted to hookers.

My dad? My dad is definitely addicted to hookers. But he's cheap.

How old is your dad?

I'm not talking about my dad.

Do brown people call their dads Dad?

I have her nipples in my mouth one after another and her breasts are huge beautiful things like the sun, each shaped perfectly, and she asks if they're the biggest I've ever seen. I say yes, which is not true, and I say they're the nicest too, which is truthful and resentful. She's been very complimentary about my cock. She asks me to get behind her and her mattress is soft and my knees dig in and my thumb begins to circle her asshole and she grabs my hand and moves the fingers to her face and has me tuck them inside her mouth and hook her cheek. This kind of violence I understand as intimacy, always. We hear her roommate clump home.

He's a DJ.

Oh yeah?

He comes home late. Don't worry, he'll be fucked up.

I don't think I'm going to cum.

Really? She isn't disappointed. She wants a task.

I'm drunk.

You are.

I don't know.

I straddle her stomach. Her breasts shift to the sides and she wraps her hand around my cock and urges me on, please? A dash of cum splatters onto her skin.

Am I the first white girl you've slept with?

Uh.

Oh—Anna.

You're not even the first brunette.

Don't be mean.

Are there different types of Hare Krishnas?

Stop it. Do you, like, pray five times a day?

Let's not.

Do you want to talk about Anna?

Not ... not really.

Sorry—was that weird? We're friends?

That was fine.

Do you have a cigarette?

I quit.

Was that weird? I'm sorry.

It's all good. Did you know Anna?

No. Sylvia told me. How long had you guys been broken up?

One year. I decide that's a better story than six months ago.

That's not long. I mean, you guys were together forever, right?

Yeah.

I have a boyfriend.

What?

I have a boyfriend.

Right now?

Yeah.

For real?

He's in Korea.

Teaching?

Yeah.

Is this okay?

Of course.

You're cute.

I am.

How can I spend fifty dollars on gin and tonics and, still, sleep doesn't come? I lazily move to eat Kali out, and we both cum again, me first, in her mouth, and then her after, her body stuttering to its own rhythm: I don't think I did much; my tongue sort of just provided an appropriate texture. She drinks most of my cum but exits for the shower to wash me off from earlier, dried now on her skin. Some of it has flaked off. I can watch the moon from her window, and she asks me if I want to spend the night or go home and I say I'll spend the night. I want to pretend to take care of someone. I want to watch the sun glow stronger and stronger and change the colours of the world black and blue to amber and red.

Melissa has a shorter haircut than before and purple lipstick that matches the red walls. She has some of it shaved and I can see her skin. It's an undercut bob thing. I'm staring at it and watching her move through our kitchen with her muscles shifting overtime.

Where's Bala at? Someone is in the basement and the smell of flesh moves through the air. This is raw, though, raw meat guts I'm smelling. Smell so strong like my nose is pulling it into me. I look down the stairs and see his brown hand flash and hear the tearing noise the dull knife makes against flesh. He's pulling the meat apart, basically. It's a pig.

Yo Bala.

No answer.

Yo Bala. You need help?

No answer.

My station has been rearranged. Where are my onions at? My knife? I don't bring my own knife to the kitchen, but there is one here I prefer to use. It has a brown handle. I've held it so many times I can feel its presence in my hand when I make a fist. It belongs to Bala, I think, and he told me to use it. The last time I saw it he was swiping it against the knife pole to maintain its edge. He moved it carelessly, even though a small slip could open him up.

Where my onions?

What? Harley says.

What is all this?

It's always like this.

No knife, no onions.

Is Sachiv in? Those woks are dirty.

No answer.

Omar, we're changing the eggs.

Melissa looks at me with wild blue eyes. She has on a plaid shirt with a grey camisole underneath. Her collarbone looks like it's going to break through the skin it's so sharp. I can't stop staring at the whiteness of her skin, the way it looks stretched to its fullest extent. She has the bare minimum of skin possible.

How do you change eggs?

You know how we roll the omelettes on top of the salsa?

Sure.

Now it's going to be salsa on the side. And the parsley in the middle of the egg, with the cheese melting in. The salsa isn't letting the cheese melt.

Our pay is three days late.

I know.

The top of my head fucks up with annoyance. I'm holding two knives now, which is an accident I don't mean to be doing, and clench. Her goofy husband is in the background making Caesars and licking his fingers clean. He's wearing a leather jacket. I'm surprised he doesn't dye his hair; blurry grey streaks snipe through long hair combed back to hide a bald spot. I want to go ruffle his hair and show off the circle of skin he's concealing. How much English do my co-workers speak? Could they fight their way to a paycheque?

Yo, wassup? Harley and his startling whiteness. He breaks boxes. We got all those tortillas, you know. Now we Latinos. Eggies in tortillas. He pronounces the word with the L's intact. He's so happy today. He has one earbud in. He's wearing a black T-shirt.

Where's my knife?

Shit, I don't know. Don't be such a bitch.

I slap Harley—a fleshy open-handed rebuke.

Harley holds his cheek. I don't think in pain because I didn't slap him that hard. I slapped him the way I used to be slapped: the way my Abu used to, with a swing loaded in anger. I slap him again.

Don't talk to me like that.

Relax man, relax.

I don't want to, but I slap him again. I crowd him into the freezer. Harley almost falls, stumbling over the slight curb that introduces the cold room. The door shuts behind us. Our breath is visible in the cold air. The shelves are lined with fish, bread, some premade sauces. You can't open the door easy; it has a special knob you have to turn. Or it can be opened from the outside. Something like euphoria cranks in me as I stand over him, and Harley lowers his body, his hands up near his face.

Don't talk to me like that. I whip my hand back but don't follow through.

Okay, man! Fucking relax!

Harley paralyzes at my violence. He could swing at me. I am not that threatening—my arms are down now, loose. I put my hand on his jaw and cheeks and clutch him tightly. I can feel his bottom teeth through his mouth flesh, I am holding on so tight. I can squeeze his teeth out.

I let him go and walk away. I have an overlap of feelings I'm not used to: the quick shock of realizing I could enact violence on someone, giddiness, and then the warble of guilt, that I am like everyone else, that Harley, crumbling in the corner, afraid, doesn't deserve this, not really. I want to say: Sorry, my body is out of my control, a ghost has taken over forever. More than I want to say sorry, though, I'm pleased with my disruption to the world, that I could still have an impact on another person, and that my slap proved that the world existed outside my brain.

The celery has to be cut and I jam my knife into my thumbnail while trying to do this. No blood yet.

Harley is in today because Sachiv called in sick, so fuck him: I fling the knife into the pit. I go to the customer bathroom. Lunch service has started. Melissa is looking for me, and the waiters have stopped still—the entire restaurant is a pool of standing water. Two men are in the bathroom, which is barely big enough. I wash with soap. I wrap a paper towel around my hand.

Omar? Omar are you in there? She calls me out. Melissa has a stack of bills. Twenties.

What?

Did you slap Harley?

Who?

Harley!

Yeah.

Why?

I have nothing to say. She fires me. I'm elated and she isn't wrong. She fires me and gives $500, which I'm not sure is right, but it's cash, so it means no deductions. She asks me to return the apron. The shirt is mine and I wear it out the back door. The lump of cash is not very thick and I know somewhere in me that this is bad.

I don't go through my cupboards to see what I have left of beans and noodles and rice. I open the freezer and take a spoon of Nathan's organic vanilla bean ice cream. I take two more spoonfuls. I needed the job, of course. I shouldn't tell Matthew about this.

I stack the twenties on my desk into not-that-high a bundle. Five hundred is not a lot. I go to the bank to deposit them; but instead, I take $300, pay my rent (I will slip the money under Nathan's door; the patter of fucking still trembling out), and change my remaining $200 to fives. The teller is reluctant to do this; I want to tell him that I've slapped a man for the first time in my life, that I've wrought abuse upon someone. Harley was scared of me. I think about him paralyzed on the freezer floor, his instincts gone, his soul abandoning him. He was left for dead. I could have killed him. I don't think he'll call the police for fear of being labelled a pussy. What is it in me that reached out to bang him like that? The flesh-on-flesh contact still darting through my body. I can't get the feeling of his skin off my hand. The $200 in fives looks larger on my desk than the twenties did. I peel the guilt away like flesh from bone.

My house has a few things from Kali. A cami and an assortment of hairpins. I don't know what to do with the clothes girls leave behind. I sniff the cami and am relieved it has no scent. I have a small drawer in my desk full of hairpins that I have collected without intent. Every time I find a hairpin on the floor of my room, or caught in my jacket, or, most often, in my bedsheet, I drop it in this drawer without thinking. If I could identify the origin of each hairpin, I would have a complete history of myself.

Kali comes out of my bathroom wearing a tank top and a pair of my boxer briefs. An empty tent of cloth where my cock and balls usually are. She told me that my dick looks like a breathing eggplant. I called her and said I wanted to celebrate, and that what I wanted to celebrate was a surprise; I have nothing to say. She kisses me where I'm at my desk on Reddit detailing how it would be useless to attack a small Atlantic town and the option to go for is the vicarious centre of Canada, Toronto, and that you could do it as easily as Timothy McVeigh did. Roll up with a truck bomb. She slides her hands onto my jeans. I had brought her flowers, a small bouquet wrapped in brown paper, mostly long stems with green leaves lying on each other. A few yellow and white petals that have already begun to lose colour. Her cheeks bloomed red when I gave them to her. I think I overstepped. She didn't look me in the eyes and flustered around my room, searching for somewhere to put them.

I can't believe you went to work this morning.

I know.

You smell like a deep fryer.

We had a french fry–heavy day.

Did you bring any home?

She likes to joke. Her boyfriend does not joke much. My phone buzzes with a message from Matthew. I close the browser window, but my computer lags, so Kali sees the post before it shuts down.

What's that, dude?

What?

Did that say bomb?

No, what?

Kali yanks back. I grab her wrists and look into her face. It's the shape of a heart and beauty marks are crammed all over it.

It's nothing. I promise.

Dude, you have to be careful.

It's whatever.

Are you being healthy?

Yo, are you a grief counsellor?

What is this macho front?

Oh, don't start with me.

Be nice.

You don't want to be a thing. I don't want to—

You can talk to me.

Are we going to be a ...

What?

Nothing.

I'm trying to have a normal friendship thing with you.

I'm not.

You want this to be what then?

I don't know. Why we doing this? Do you miss me?

Excuse me?

Do you?

Yes.

You do. Then? That means—

I mean—I miss everyone.

What does that mean.

I love everyone, you know. I try to live like that.

What?

I don't think it's finite. Love. It grows.

What?

You only love a few people?

Not ... why are we talking about love?

Relax.

Jeez.

Let's relax.

Do you want more?

I miss you. Isn't that enough?

I didn't say I want more.

It's okay if you want more.

Easy. I did not say that.

Are we cool?

I'm practised at weaponizing my sadness while evading it. She has tiny feet that don't match her long body and little pouches of fat on each hip. I tell her I can trace the constellations on her moles and she tells me I'm a dumb-ass. I ask her to put her feet in my mouth and she obliges and I work over each toe while she masturbates. Sleep is begging me to come to it.

You okay?

I don't really like feet. She tugs hers away fast. I mean, you have nice feet—I don't *like like* feet, you know?

I didn't know you were going to—

Would you put my feet in your mouth?

Socrates asked me to marry him.

What?

My boyfriend.

From Korea?

I think he was serious.

His name is Socrates?

He's half-Greek.

Why are all these half people so obsessed with their non-white side?

He didn't name himself Socrates.

Do you call him Sock?

He's my fiancé now.

Really?

Really.

Really really?

Really really really.

You're E-engaged.

He wants to open a bar here. He wants to save money for it.

I'll come.

You're not invited.

It'll be a big space. You won't notice me. I can cook.

I don't want you there. You're not invited.

What if we become friends?

We are friends.

Me and Sock, I mean.

I don't think so.

He sounds smart.

Socrates wants to be serious.

You're so beautiful.

Omar.

When's he back?

In six months.

I have six months.

This isn't practical now. I'm engaged.

You have a ring?

He's saving for it.

Why do you want to be engaged to him?

I love him.

Why are you doing this?

This is fun.

Oh.

You're sweet. I like you.

Wow.

This can be like, fun, and meaningful. It can be like a thing. It doesn't have to be a forever thing to be meaningful.

You're engaged now.

Right. He's not here.

And you want me to not be ... engaged.

I want you to be engaged. Is this confusing?

What do you want?

What do you want?

This is the worst conversation.

I'm sorry. I thought—we can stop.

No, no. I didn't say that.

Are you sure?

I try to respect boundaries.

I'm being respectful!

You're pushy.

You're not, like, human.

Is that an okay thing to say?!

I'm teasing.

Does Sock know about us?

We see other people.

I don't think that's what I asked.

What does it matter?

It's important to me.

Why?

Because. I want him to know.

He doesn't know about you, specifically, no. He doesn't want to. He doesn't need to.

Will you tell him?

No.

For me?

No.

Is he more important to you than me?

Jesus. Omar—stop.

So, we're nothing.

We're not nothing.

But you ain't posting me on Facebook.

Omar.

So I have six months.

I lie on top of her and we kiss until I'm hard and she's wet and she inserts two fingers into my mouth as I push into her. We stay like that until I cum and she takes her fingers out and finishes herself while I'm soft in her, slowly falling out.

She begins to fill me in on Sock's plan to move back. She shows me a text with an image of the kind of wood he wants to use in the place for tables or chairs or whatever. The text after that: *I love you. 180 sleeps!* There's a great fear in my chest when I read these texts, and I move the sheets off my body. It's too hot. It's too hot to read, I say. I want to grab her and throw the phone out the window. Of course. My heart is running so fast I'm going to puke it up. I get out of bed and pace, fully aware of how shrieking crazy I must seem. I pretend to fiddle with my phone. I can't stop myself from moving back and forth across the room. My body is building a froth of heat inside it. I don't know what to do with this heat; I'm not feeling angry, or turned on, I can feel these gunshot vibrations of energy. She's scrolling through something on her phone.

Most restaurants fail.

It's going to be a bar.

I want drastic failure in Sock's future.

Kali pats the bed for me to come sit. Stop being dumb. Come sit down.

I walk her back to her place on Brunswick Avenue, past the crumbling student houses and the fat brownstone mini mansions. Another Chinese-looking lady rifling through recycling. I see her all the way down the street in front of a small mansion with two empty bottles of wine. She finds a pack of six brown beer bottles, a six-pack of green bottles, six clear bottles. She rearranges her cart and slides them all in, thin crinkling noises. I smile at her when I pass and she nods. Students are good for something when they leave the bottles out for her. The sun is crackling in the air, my breath fresh—I feel okay. Kali's taste and the memory of the way her belly curved when she lay on her side thrum through me. On College Street a condo development has slowly been building towards the sky for months now, building and building, reaching for the moon and clouds that we're not going to get to. I asked my father way before: What happens when we die? How can heaven work if we all die at different ages? He told me that a person is all different ages in heaven and that you see them at their best age. I try not to think about Anna up there from four years ago. Four years ago we had a month without a fight, a month of no fighting that I ruined by mentioning we had not fought. She told me fighting was her nature, and how could I get mad at someone for their nature? That month was all fucking, no squabbles.

A cop redirects me off the sidewalk with a nod. They're taking the crane down. A section of the street is portioned off and each piece of the crane is disassembled and piled onto a flatbed. Eight or ten people are helping, and an extra man with video equipment is recording everything. He's wearing a yellow hard hat and the construction workers are wearing white ones. He has the nicest jeans on. Behind him is a camera bag, two cameras, two lenses, and other equipment I don't recognize. There is a policeman at the other end with his back to me. The cop I passed now has his back to me too; the workers have their backs to me. The sun slips past the clouds and illuminates the bag—everything is coated in bright yellow light banking off snow. I snatch up a camera, click the lens off, and shove it into my jacket. Time widens. I fast-walk down Augusta, into the market until I reach Dundas. I get onto a streetcar and go east, towards a pawnshop I remember.

Today is the funeral. Anna is a rock in the river and people are gushing around her body. Her body is on display again, like at the viewing. I will have to look at her. Why don't we just throw people into the ground? Anna was careful about this, talking to me about cremation and being burned all the way through the bones. She wanted to be wisps of smoke disappearing into air. She wanted to control her death—cancer, disease—to prepare boxes for her ashes. You have to control your demise, she said. Ashes and flowers—use me to plant a garden, or better yet, use me for some food, mingled with tomato seedlings, please. She loved dirt, crumbled soil, wet mud, muck under her fingernails.

Her hands folded over her hips in the rectangular wooden box, the cross. I should have told Bernie that Anna wanted to be burned up. Don't they already know? Emina said something. Why is she in this box? One last look. I tried to speak to her, to him, to someone who was related to her, and the words formed in my throat but stopped themselves from birthing at my lips. Why is she in a box? She looks like she was painted on. What is this look? This is Friday nightclub land makeup, not easy Sunday morning brunch. She looks like she was painted for the prowl. Or not—she never wore heavy makeup. Or I never saw her in it; this is a new Anna. I'm startled by her appearance, how she could look so different, so new, how there is still a part of her I have not seen.

Her fingers are unpolished, except for the left thumb, where they've left chipped freckles of baby blue. The sweater is too thick for the funeral home. The casket has two sorts of lids, and the one over her legs is closed. You can't see into it because of the white fluff, almost a blanket, that presses down above her knees and recedes into darkness. What kind of shoes is she going to be wearing into the ground?

I move closer to her—a railing lines the casket—noise goes down a notch; everyone knows I'm going to kiss her? Up close, the skin looks right, deflated, but right. She never wore any perfume and the taxidermist or whoever gets that part right. The tangled smell of weed that sometimes followed her is missing, and that's what I miss now: interacting with her bad habits, her drunk spells, her stoner clarity, the slowed-down gaze. She smells like clothes soap.

My ear to her heart. She's wearing a pair of her blue pants. Professional pants. I rest for five, six, seven beats, pushing my head into her chest. The brim of her blue pants around the belt, and I can see a slice of the light blue underwear chosen for her. Her stomach hairs are flat. A slip of skin showing between her shirt and pants the width of a nickel. Socks? Shoes? Changing her like she's a live baby. I couldn't finish my eggs this morning. The shaky white perimeters reminding me of babies again. Wiggling like a chicken trying to reconstitute itself, cracking on the hot black flat pan. I undercooked them, and the whites were goopy, drained through the buckteeth of my fork and hit my plate.

I know she is not to be buried in that casket, but I can't remove the thought of the lid opening and closing on her like an eager jaw. I miss my body, slapping Harley. I miss its force, its craziness, the machinery of it. I see the mahogany richness of wood splinter and split, trying to chew Anna's body. I know she will be cremated; I know she will not be lowered into the ground to rot in a box. I see the pulp of her body mushed by the casket teeth. I think about slapping Harley again. I wish Anna had slapped me a few more times so I could have the experience solidly in my head. If reincarnation turns out to be a thing, I'll remind her. I was supposed to be scared slapping Harley while the consequences were simultaneously running through my head. All I felt was this lush joy that comes from knowing yourself. It was the same way I felt with Anna at our highest pitch, when the shriek of a mind is silenced and you're left with your body. To feel my blood flowing through me, threatening to gush out of my skin—this is a gift Harley gave me. I feel overworn with gratitude. I want to sleep, finally.

I wish I had taken a photograph of Harley crouched in the freezer. I will lose its shape and it'll disappear, hopefully not before I can get meaning from it. I keep mishandling and forgetting epiphanies—I swear I could understand once before why Anna had kept me hidden from her family. She had explained it to me, explained upsetting them, and I understood that that was bad, and it did soothe, even if it was wrong. I understood how I might serve as a respite from the terror they brought her and that I shouldn't ask so many questions. I was wrong to think love meant inclusion, instead of protection from the shrill terror of life. It was subtle, but they were different. She was right.

This morning I'm in North York again. I've never wanted to come back, but I felt like walking around. I decide to visit Ami and Abu, maybe tell them about Anna, see if they remember her (of course they would). The 96 wobbles into Graydon Hall. There's no bars or anything around here, and the five buildings (20, 50, 75 [a condo], 100, 150) stutter one after another in a line over a kilometre. Houses are on either side and the neighbourhood is wild—Pakis and Persians before; now it's stunned full of Chinese and Koreans. Two shiny buildings, 2020 and 2060, are across Don Mills, and where all the Jamaican kids I knew lived. I had a friend there, Brandon, a skinny, tall, menacing kid, who was quiet like drizzle, who stood at the lockers and didn't bug no one. I called him once in grade four and his father picked up and said one word: Speak. I was so scared I hung up. I think I see him sometimes downtown working the door at College Street bars, but I don't speak to him.

I call Hussain halfway there because I realize this is stupid—what does nostalgia get me? I remember praying at a mosque once, bent over, prostrated, at mercy, the quiet swallow of the world overtaking me. The church yesterday was the same, for a snatch second. The snow has been coming down in pounds, kilos, tons, fluttered and flaked, demented. Like staring into a real-life dead channel. I stop at the tuck shop, avoiding 20 Graydon Hall and my folks in apartment 908.

I see Hussain, fresh fade, awkward gait like a bird. He's wearing a green jacket, Timbs, cargo pants, and he smells like cherry cigarillos. There's something handsome about him. The way his fake gold hangs off his neck, the silver nubs in his ear. Sometimes he wore a ring: I remember in high school he knocked this kid Jamal on the forehead and the ring gashed. They rolled down a small hill and both broke bones—Hussain his ankle, Jamal his hand on Hussain's head. We talked about who won that fight for days while both were suspended.

Bruh. Hussain pretends to dig a gun into my kidney. I freeze when he bucks up against me like that and the fear straightens my spine. Chill, you dumb fuck. What're you saying up here?

Visiting my folks.

They still at Graydon Hall?

Where else? I thumb the small nugget of weed in my pocket: Matthew's. These kids hate each other—Matthew so buff now, though. I wish Matthew was here, all chiselled out after four years of university gym. Hussain's Timbs are scuffed and dirty. Matthew's small suede brush in his pocket. What would I do if Hussain tried to take the weed off me? Matthew still doesn't know how to fight, no matter how often he goes into that mixed martial arts gym. He told me that the anxiety slows him down and he can't get used to the violence, that he has to stop going because he can't avoid sparring anymore. He works the bag over and over again. Hussain moves with violence. He's chubby since high school, a ring of fat across his belly and dark patches sagging under his eyes, but tension still furious in him. Hussain looks like he has given himself a haircut; the taper is all fucked up. He notices me looking and rubs the back of his head. His clothes are old too.

Say you're my manager.

Nah, man.

Why not?

What if you get caught or something?

They're not gonna know, eh?

Are they gonna call or email me?

Call. You good for cash? You sell those Yeezys?

Not yet.

Remember that Sam kid?

From school?

Remember when we taxed him for his Xbox and PlayStation?

From his house, right? When his parents were gone.

I got another thing like that.

What is it?

There's a house down the road. Andrew.

I remember that kid.

His mom is a surgeon. I dunno when they're gone, but he was saying that they go on vacation a lot. They got a big house.

He still lives with his parents?

He a bum. Let's do it.

Do what?

I dunno, man, they got a nice place. I need to take a few things.

Nah, that's wild.

Why not?

Who knows what kinda security they have?

Security ain't nothing. An alarm blah blah and then we bounce.

I got a better thing. I surprise myself.

You do?

This girl I'm seeing. I watch myself talk to Hussain.

She got a connect?

Nah, her roommate. He's a producer.

Oh shit ...

He's got a wild set-up—recording equipment, microphones, turntables and shit. I know where the key is. I don't know him. I've never even seen him. My whole life feels like a hallucination of choices. I can give my rot away.

In and out.

Easy.

Damn.

In high school we stole Sam's video game stuff, on a dare mostly, adrenaline gunning through us. I swear this kid Mo said Bismillah before we went in. We rumbled through the living room on our tiptoes, trying not to let each other hear the blood going mad in us. All we managed was a PlayStation, Xbox, and some games. Hussain sold the PlayStation, gave me fifty bucks. I have no idea how much it was worth. His skin is looser now, eleven years later, but he is jumpy, still ready to leave his body and ascend. He is desperate. He has a kid, a two-year-old, with a girl named Cassandra, I think. She had a ponytail that hung down to her lower back, had been growing it forever. He starts talking about alligators on a recent trip to Florida and the way that it blew up his Visa. He has two kids, not one, Sonia and Mirelle, both with Cassandra. I ask if Cassandra still has her ponytail, and he glares at me sharp. I think about life in that small North York apartment and the rumpled structure his day-to-day has taken on. Anna would ask about this: How would we live if we had kids? She rarely let me cum inside her, and when I would ask coyly, while fucking, pretending to be in the throes but deliberate, she refused and would tell me after, in bed, her legs refusing to tangle with mine, that I wasn't ready. That I wouldn't be able to take care of anyone or anything, so why should she let me? When we were drunk she would forget this and tear into my back, grind her legs with mine, and beg me to cum in her. Then she would rush to the toilet after to squat, evacuating my sperm out of her. It hurt, the way she quickly rushed to make sure there was no trace of me in her (she was on the pill, even), but I never let her know.

A'ight, you wanna do it?

Let's do it tonight.

For real?

She works tonight and he's at a gig.

I don't want to tell my parents anything. I leave North York as I came, on the bus, without speaking to them.

Hussain has a bottle of Iceberg cranked open and he dips the vodka into a Coke bottle.

There's a can in the back, eh, but it's warm.

I open the can and pour half of it outside the window.

You gonna turn the heat on?

Nah.

Nah?

It don't work. Thanks for doing this.

All good.

I spent some money I shouldn't have.

Florida, yeah.

Cassandra, you know. Her mom moved to Thunder Bay. So

we had some money saved so she could fly there with Sonia and Mirelle.

It's not actually that cold tonight, but sitting in the car is. The vodka stings. We're tucked away at College and Spadina, next to a florist. Cars zoom in and out. It's 8:45 p.m. Why are we meeting so early?

I wanna go to this party. You wanna come?

Nah.

You got a thing after?

Nah.

No white girl hanging around?

Nah.

He laughs. Sorry, yo, Cassie white. I shouldn't talk.

You been with Cassandra for enough time.

My parents asked her to come to the mosque.

For real?

It was a'ight. My mom is tight with her now. Since Sonia. She dropped all the nonsense.

That's good. For the kids.

You know. It's good for me, man. Makes life easier.

What'd you do with the money?

Nothing, really. Spent it. Clothes. I mean, I'm working. I said I been working at that bar, Crowns, under the table. Cassie came in the other day—damn. I had no idea. She gave the girls to my mom and she came in to surprise me. Wanted to have a drink while I was the bartender. She fucking popped off. Brad, the guy that owns the place, he's straight. He stood up and said I worked there but must have gotten the schedule messed up. I guess it's good that he lied for me and all, but then she was hollering at me, asking where the fuck I was when I said I was gonna be there.

Where were you?

Nowhere, man. I was at Rutchit's playing Xbox. I wasn't doing shit. You know how much energy it takes to get a sidepiece now? To hide all that? I did it once, four years ago. I had this Filipino girl, but man, she wanted so much. She wanted to be my girl, you know, not someone I fucked and then dipped. I couldn't handle. She was beautiful but yo, I couldn't handle it. Rutchit was like, Yo yo yo, get another phone, get a prepaid, but it's like, where the fuck do I keep that phone? What the fuck happens if Cassandra finds that phone? I can't keep that shit straight. It's work too, for what? For a nut? You gotta put work in. It's dating. I ain't about that. All my money gone—I have two babies.

That why you end it?

Nah, Cassandra found out. Rutchit had an extra phone, he lent it to me, I left it in the glove compartment. Got pulled over one day and reached for registration and phone drops out. Cop on my left asking me about priors and Cassie screaming at me on my right and Sonia and Mirelle in the back crying and I had smoked one too, so, man, I was halfway done. I dunno how the cop didn't scope that shit out. I'm sitting in the middle and everyone yelling at me. I told Rutchit and he laughs. He's got two girls—he still with Tashelle—Tashelle! From way back! Plus he got that job, plus he got Xbox, plus he got time for me and a weekly bowl, plus he got his kids, who don't hate him. Two kids. Tashelle pregnant too. He made.

Hussain finishes his bottle and turns the ignition. The Acura sputters and the lights blink on and we're on College and then on Brunswick Street.

I got this computer thing too. Trying to sell computers. You remember Aman?

With the fucked-up teeth?

That homie. He got his hands on all these computers and he wants me to help him sell them. For five bills or something. They're IBM or whatever. We put them on Craigslist and they gone like that.

The street is cricket quiet. I poured too much Coke out, too much vodka in.

You watch that video?

Yeah.

And?

And what? It was fucked up.

Nah, man. It's legit.

Bruh, I don't wanna watch people getting their heads cut off. Forget that.

That's what it was.

The reason, man. It made sense.

Bro—

Fighting back, right?

Since when you give a shit?

I have kids, man. They half-white, but they brown.

So?

If we don't do nothing?

You gonna join ISIS after we done here?

Bro. Hussain kisses his teeth. Cassie got me protesting. She taking it serious. All these white converts be hyped up politically. More than us.

Us.

Yeah man, us.

They're like born-agains.

They straight.

What you gonna do?

Nothing ... I dunno ... Raise my kids ... That video didn't make you think?

Think about what, man? Shit's fucked up. I ain't part of that life—that ain't on me.

You can do other shit.

I ain't got time.

Cassie out next week marching.

It's too cold for that.

Donate some cash.

I ain't been to a mosque in a minute.

Yo: the stats in the vid. A hundred thousand Afghans dead. Five hundred thousand in Syria. Fifty thousand in Yemen.

What you want me to do? Go over there? I raise my voice, looking at Hussain, wanting him to stop this line of questions.

You don't wanna do anything?

I ain't there. I'm here. By myself. What you doing?

Don't worry about me right now. We gotta get you into a mosque first. Get you around your people.

Yeah, my people. Your wife wear a niqab? I cut the tension, careful not to cross Hussain's see-saw line.

Man, shut the fuck up. Hussain laughs. We'll put you in with the converts. Get you a Bosnian. Hussain drinks the last of the vodka Coke and coughs. You been to this house before?

Yeah.

What we gonna do?

Honestly, not much. Key is under a potted plant or some dumb shit. In, out. I peeked in his room—MacBook, whole bunch of recording shit, I don't know what the fuck it is. Looks expensive.

A'ight. I'll stay downstairs, you go up to his room and grab whatever.

The house right there.

Hussain hits the brake hard. He wraps a scarf around his face. You done this since Sam?

Nah.

Be easy. Walk up like it's yours.

You got a scarf?

Nah, don't worry about it. Don't buck your head around. All the neighbours don't know shit. Be easy, that's it.

We exit the car and he closes his door soft, and I slam mine trying to be natural. There's no gate to the front door, and he leads. I lift the first pot and see there's nothing. The front door is green and has a noisy screen, I remember. Have I entered here sober? I start panicking at the lack of key and whip my head around—there are some cars, but no one in them that I can see. One in the distance that looks like it has two people chatting in it, or eating, or something—a black smear. I quick squint to see if it's that cop, but shadows are dark and lying over everything. It couldn't be. We talked about all this in person, nothing over the internet or on the phone. Unless they're following me, still?

Hussain moves quick, no fluttering, lifting up the Welcome mat and then two potted plants before he finds it. He opens the door, turns on his cell light, and raises his finger to his lips to signal me quiet. I'm not used to the layout—I usually walk through drunk and straight to Kali's room. Thinking about it slows me down. There's the first stairs, then the living room, kitchen, and two bedrooms, Kali's farthest away. We creep up and he points me to the back. There's no light in this house, the moon is gone, and I've forgotten my cellphone in the car. Or did it fall out of my pocket? I pat myself down all over, but no luck. Hussain is not standing still; he moves to the back, and I thought he was supposed to wait? The beam of his cellphone guides him into Kali's room and I follow him. Hussain is tumbling through her room. He's not fear or shadow; he is violence: He possesses a will I'm learning about. He moves like he's never had a past. He uses both eyeballs separately, I swear. I'm overjoyed that this has gone too far. I don't want him to stop. I have to act when I think of him vandalizing the room I spend time in.

Yo, what the fuck? A tight whisper from me.

Don't worry. He strips her pillows of their cases and gives one to me. I head to her roommate's room and turn the light on: fuck. The window faces the street. Shut the blinds. All his expensive shit is laid out. Dude has a lot of cologne. I drop two watches, a rack full of chains, and some rings into the case. I see four boxes of Nikes. I take a look and they're beautiful, but what am I doing? I slide in his MacBook, what looks like some recording gear, a little MIDI keyboard.

Hussain is at the door: Yo, don't forget the cords.

What cords?

There are eight hundred cords in a mess on the floor.

Forget that.

I can't sell it without the cords.

Put it on Kijiji, man, someone will buy it.

Hussain walks into the room, bends over near the desk, pulls the power bar out off the wall, and tugs the whole thing into a pillowcase. The stereo collapses.

Let's bounce.

He has a full case.

What's in there?

She had some nice shit.

Yo, what? I put my hand on him.

I took a little jewellery and a laptop. That's it.

Nah, man, not cool.

This ain't enough. You said he had way more shit. That's nothing. He pushes past me and we exit the way we came in, replace the key, and try not to speed-walk to the car. Let's go let's go let's go.

The people are still chatting in their car.

Fuck.

We good. We good. That was a good haul.

How we gonna split this up?

I'll sell this and give you cash.

Nah, give me her shit.

Fuck that, man.

Nah, gimme her shit. I'll sell it.

Are you dumb? You gonna give it back to her?

You can't rob her, man!

It's done. It's jewellery.

And the MacBook and shit? How we gonna cut that in half?

So what you wanna do? Let me sell it and I'll give you the cash when I see you next. I told you.

We're moving way out of downtown now.

Where you going?

Home.

I live downtown.

You wanna get out?

We're on the fucking highway.

A'ight, I'll get off at the exit and you can peace.

Where the fuck are we?

Get a cab.

Take me to a subway.

I gotta get Cassie for this party.

Take me to a subway.

Yo, you're pissing me off, eh?

Homie, I robbed a house with you. Gimme that fucking shit.

Who the fuck you talking to?

Drive me to the subway.

Hussain slows and gets off the highway. I don't know where we are. The car stops. His hand erupts and snaps against the side of my head. I was tense and ready for it—I was ready for it this entire time—and I'm already moving away as the fist flashes towards me. He still hits me, and I smash my head against the window. My seat belt is on and I can't get it off. He hits me again and again: my jaw, my shoulder. I swing once and hit him in the mouth; I'm not sure it hurts him, but I cut my knuckle on his teeth.

You bitch ass.

I grab a pillowcase, and stumble out of the car. Hussain reverses—I jump out of the way of his pretty good three-point turn—and he's gone.

I look in the bag—Kali's shit.

Kali texts me twice, but I don't answer. I read them again and again. They are simple:

u up
come over
i'll be home in 20
helloooo
fu
jk
glad u got some sleep J

And then:

holy shit r u up?
we got robbed
george is freaking out
the cops are here

I don't sleep. I sit on my bed and try to figure out what happened and how one event clapped into another. I am only a ghost being pulled along through events. At four a.m. I'm walking around College Street, and I see Sylvia in a black dress. What's the difference between a ghost and a soul? Sylvia is one, I am the other. We're in a tuck shop together. She's buying munchies. A silver belt hanging loose on her hips. She's drunk with friends and I try to see if Matthew is there, or anyone I know, but no one. The fluorescents are radiant like sun, and how is it possible that only one person feels a connection? Does Kali feel too much for me? How does she manage to have feelings for me and Sock? I am drunk on this no-sleep, so I hide near the chocolates and watch Sylvia pay for a pack of Belmonts. I've never seen her smoke. She looks lovely: her shoulder blades rippling like wings. It's okay then, I realize, that I think about her in cliché. I don't know her. I'm leaning too hard on some display and the Mars fall. I don't immediately turn to address them and see her flinch to turn towards the crash, but she stops her entire body—she knows it's me. She has a sense. She fights against the instinct to look towards the noise. She doesn't want to make eye contact. That's okay. I say that out loud, I think. That's okay. I can see her in the security mirror above the cash register. She must be able to see me in there too, and I swear she looks up occasionally to make eye contact, but that's not true. Once she pays for the cigarettes, I watch her clack out. Her heels are purple soled and they remind me of sour candies melting on my tongue. Her knees are a little dry and I think I can see tangles of white dry skin spiralling down towards her shins like she was dipped in white glue. I think maybe I should go ask her for a cigarette and pretend I don't know her. Can only one person be in love out of two? If you're a proper couple, you're one.

Sylvia moves towards a side street and I cling to my Red Bull while taking bites of a Mars bar. She walks a bit bowlegged, her ankles tired after a long night. She must be drunk. Maybe she went home with someone else. Where is the sun? She lives west but is walking east. I watch her move farther and farther away; I slow my pace and decide to hail a cab for her. I dry heave a bit, in a very controlled, professional way, three loud gasps, like a hand is pulling the air out of me. My stomach is sore—I did not work out—each ab in raw pain. Tangled in my impulses: leave Sylvia alone, try to atone for being myself, lead her into a cab, put my arm around her, and sneak her back into my apartment, lick the underside of her thighs, stuff her into a black garbage bag with myself, seal that bag up and fall asleep on her chest while the air whimpers out. I finish the chocolate bar, hail a cab, babble in Hindi while pointing to Sylvia. The driver looks at me and follows my finger. He has the tidiest cab I've ever seen, no road maps, no GPS, a neat photograph of his unsmiling face, a long set of beads hanging from the rear-view mirror. He moves the car forward and honks at Sylvia. She looks at him and shakes her head no. I don't know what anyone wants, but that's okay. Matthew would say something polite like that.

Big beams of memory are gone. I barely remember Anna's funeral; I don't remember Matthew there, or anyone. I have a few hundred dollars in my dresser in a sock, in three socks. The Yeezys are gone. I fall asleep and dream of my father sitting on the top of a mountain while the sun melts. He speaks down to me, the beggar at the cusp, waiting for wisdom, but the sun melts and pours into me, lights me on fire from the inside.

Nights keep passing without any input. I've been in this apartment for a year now. It has a gas stove and blue light rolls under the pan when I click it on. I'm trying to cook eggs, but while I'm forgetting what I'm looking for in the fridge, the swift smell of smoke comes alive. The pan, the oil, is superheated—a pop and a cloud and flame swells on the surface. I grab the handle and open the window and hold the weapon outside. Raindrops hiss on the pan, and the flames won't go out, so I drop it all the way down to the ground. It rolls a bit before it settles. Enough heat that the rain is still cooking when it hits, but the noise gets quieter and quieter, then the fire is gone and there's only smoke: so much smoke.

When I look across the black of the bar I can find the body that looks the most like Anna's. There's one in the corner next to two guys playing pool, both with mega arms and fades and veins like cords. They are both wearing all black, and she is wearing a purple dress and sipping from a gin and tonic. The guys have bottles of beer. The ball drops into the pocket consistently. Thock thock thock. Matthew is across from me. We aren't really speaking while sipping beer. The Raptors are on the screen above. Both men know what they're doing. Matthew has to be drunk by the way he's sitting. He really likes Sylvia, he tells me. He doesn't know what to do. Matthew was already a bit tipsy by the time I arrived.

The girl in the purple dress looks like she would help you if you needed it. Her skin like a white sheet and ugly in contrast to her dress. Long curly hair. I want to pull her into my arms and beg. She bothers both guys equally, taking turns talking to them.

I can't figure out if she's with either of them. She touches each of them on their shoulders and I see the muscle underneath. They're making fun of her and flirting as a unit, curling laughs out of her. At eleven, the music sharpens and she has to dig her mouth towards their ears so they can hear her. She puts her hands on their hips and talks directly into their ears. I want that wet breath on my neck. She goes to the bathroom and I think about following her. I give it serious consideration. I could stand in front of the bathroom door and think about the copper taste of the doorknob, and of her—the same taste that everyone has underneath it all.

The bar is full of dark-haired white women. I think everyone here is from U of T. Matthew's still dragging me to these university bars. I am losing him; he's the type to disappear once he has a girlfriend, to let her take all of him in.

Matthew knows the dudes playing pool and they walk over when they see him, dap, and Linda, the purple-dress girl, comes back from the bathroom and introduces herself. I want her to be a vivid replica of Anna, and when she sits down I start speaking to her and ignore the two guys. She speaks not like Anna—she swears more, she eats chicken wings, and Matthew is staring at me. The two guys look at me in a way that confirms my mania. I pick up one of her chicken wings and eat the fat, the red sauce scribbling over my fuzz and fingers, and I send psychic messages to Linda to lick them clean. I embarrass Matthew, I realize, and stop myself from taking another wing. She excuses herself to go to the bar for another drink, and her friends leave with her.

I feel like everyone has been lying to me.

What you mean?

The note.

I think people are looking out for you.

What does that mean?

Really?

Really.

You weren't ... handling the breakup well.

Yo, what was your advice? Get laid.

Did you?

A little.

Bro. Matthew is half laughing while slurping on his beer. It was like. Months of nothingness.

I was chilling.

You could see why—

Are you lying to me?

'Bout what? Doesn't everyone want you to be okay?

The note. I can't get it out of my head. Matthew is silent. He watches the Raptors on TV, staring so hard like he's counting the dribbles. What you think?

What's a note gonna say?

I dunno.

Seriously.

Sorry?

What's that gonna do?

Make me feel better?

She gone, man.

I want her to make me feel better.

I know, but—

It'll be like a thing.

What's a note gonna do? Say sorry for what? Tell you she was sad? You feel responsib—

No.

Then?

I don't not feel responsible.

Bro.

She was my ex. You know, they say "in" love, like two people be in love.

She wasn't you, though.

People keep saying that. People also say when you in love, it's that, it's that "oneness."

You not in love!

Why? 'Cause she dead?

I think so.

Nah.

Nah, what?

Nah!

How's Kali?

I dunno.

And you got fired?

Yeah, yeah.

What you doing for work?

I got money.

From what?

I got money.

Why don't you go back to George Brown, go to that cooking school?

Maybe I should become a cop.

Want me to look at your resumé?

I don't have a resumé.

You wanna ... make a resumé?

Can we just watch ball?

I'm saying I'll help.

Okay, you know, I gotta dip.

Nah, nah, nah. Take it easy.

Homie, I'm okay. I don't need to be babysat.

You can't leave me at a bar like this. I'll look weird. We have a whole pitcher.

I finish my pint and throw down a five. Matthew puts his hands on me to try to stop me, but I move them. His hands are full of blood and warm. I need to be around people who only see me from the outside.

The air is cold and shrieking. I have nowhere to go and no one to see. I head home.

There are two vampire-looking dudes in suits waiting for me on Baldwin, in front of my place.

Omar?

I look at them. Their suits are dark. One, I think, is a brown suit. The navy suit is on the brown man. They are standing in my way.

We've met. My name is Kevin Mohammad and this is Ryan—

Get out of my face.

Kevin steps in front of me and I realize he is built. He is content to not move. The air seems cooler around him, as if all warmth runs away fast.

Can you come with us?

I don't know you.

We're with the RCMP, Omar. I offered you my card.

No, you are not.

Yes. They show me identification.

Yo, what? Why you standing outside my place like a creep?

Son.

I don't know you.

Come with us.

Yo, get out of my face.

Omar Ali.

It's when he says my last name that the gears in me start crunching. Everything in my guts comes to a full stop. People I don't know shouldn't know my full name. Ryan is squat and still; he hangs near the driver's side staring at me with tiny blue eyes. Kevin Mohammad—what the fuck is that name? I'd never be able to move him. The suit is tight across his chest, and he has a pocket square and perfectly dimpled tie.

What kind of name is that?

Guyanese.

I kiss my teeth, unsure what to say.

Where we going? I don't want to talk to you.

We can arrest you.

Okay. So?

Omar. You broke into a house two nights ago.

No.

Omar, we saw it happen. On Brunswick. He chucks his head in that direction. You were with Hussain Syed.

Who?

Omar.

Their stance is weird. I know they are threatening me, but they are containing it. They want something from me; they want me. They are trying to keep it hidden. Menace comes out of Kevin's voice in dabs and drips as they try to find an entry point to me. Kevin doesn't move and I don't move and we both know I'm not moving because I'm terrified.

Get in the fucking car, Omar. Ryan speaks.

I want to go back to the bar and beg Linda for a cigarette and apologize to Matthew.

Ryan lets go of the door handle and takes a step forward. Kevin steps back and opens the back door. I get in. Inside is phantom dark, light too scared to enter.

We sit in a white-lit room. They are being kind to me, considering I do not know exactly what I'm here for and they do. I decide they're my two favourite ghouls. Their shadows stretch long against the wall, hell black against bone white. I have coffee to rub the booze off and a packet of Harvest Cheddar SunChips. Ryan asks me if chips are halal and I say that I don't know, that I don't care, and he says, Of course you don't, in a tone that means something to him and nothing to me. I'm starting to feel ill. Not because of the room but the two pints on an empty stomach. The chips aren't doing much. They make me hungrier for something substantial.

I try to ping this experience off movies I've seen, to understand how I would fit in the tradition of film. Neither of them seems to have a personality except for stern. No one has yelled. No one else is in the room. The room has no one-way mirror either but a camera mounted in the corner. The room isn't that brightly lit—actually, it's appropriately lit—and I am not in cuffs or chained down.

Kevin: Do you know why you're here?

You're bad at your job.

Ryan: You're not like Hussain, Omar. Don't be tough.

Ryan is like if stone was made into a man. His voice is wrung out and high-pitched and it's hard to take him seriously the way it trills out of his throat.

No, sir.

Why did you rob that house?

What house?

On Brunswick. We were there. You were with Hussain Syed.

Who?

Ryan: We saw you!

Okay.

How do you know Hussain?

Who?

Kevin: Omar.

Ohhhh, Hussain, you mean? I don't really.

How do you know him?

From high school? Maybe middle school. From high school.

And you rob houses often.

I've never robbed a house in my life.

You two walked right into the house.

Does that sound like a robbery? Sounds like we were let in.

Really? Would the inhabitants of the house agree?

You should ask them.

They seemed distraught.

Why'd you pick me up?

Ryan: You walked right in. You knew where the key was.

Can I get a lawyer?

Can you afford a lawyer?

Don't I get one for free?

You want them to press charges?

For what?

Omar, we saw everything happen. We saw everything from step one.

I didn't rob a house. I don't know what you saw.

Do you know a lot about Hussain?

What?

He's under a peace bond.

Okay.

Do you know why?

Why am I here? This is a weird way to arrest me for a robbery.

Because of his online activity.

Okay.

We thought he had the potential to commit terrorist offences.

Ryan's face lifts and stretches when he says this, his eyebrows to the heavens, his mouth down, low, elongating every ounce of meaning when he says the bogey word. I can't stop imagining him crushing garlic in his hands.

Okay, man, I think I'm out. Like, maybe a robbery—but this is kinda—

And Hussain gets in trouble a lot. So we've noticed him for a while.

Honestly, like, you need to—

And then you, with him, have been doing what exactly?

And me? Are you out of your mind? I'm not about to commit a terrorist offence.

Really? So why are you going online and saying you are?

(   )

You're going on Reddit saying—what? That you're going to cut off people's heads.

Nah, it's not like that.

Omar, you are not in here because we *think* you did these things. We know what you've been talking about online. Do you know what the difference is between you and Hussain?

I think you guys are fucking insa—

He's been using Twitter and WhatsApp to talk to terrorist groups overseas. ISIS, Jaish-e-Mohammed. That's it. He's communicating with terrorists in Pakistan, Afghanistan, Syria. That's the *only* difference. That's why he's under a peace bond. Why did you think this was okay?

It's a joke, man, a fucking *joke*. I live in Toronto—how the fuck am I going to cut off Trudeau's head?

I say this even though I know there is a cobweb of surveillance around the city. I know that brown men get used for this kind of churning. Their anger makes me happy; happy to be in this room, happy to see that my behaviour could have consequences, happy to see I have reach. Is this the end, or the beginning? Is this bigger than it seems, or not? I won't actually be fucked off to Syria or Oman or Saudi Arabia or some other Arab state, will I?

You joke regularly about assassinating the prime minister?

I didn't think anyone was reading it.

You posted it for people to read—to scare people.

I was dicking around.

What does this say?

Kevin slides a paper over. It's a printout of a Reddit post of mine, from when I first started, after Anna. I can't tell exactly, they're mostly the same.

This was for fun.

Ryan and Kevin stare at me. Kevin licks his lips, his tongue mimicking a snail exactly, slow, fat, slimy, almost as if he's tasting himself. He pulls his tongue back into his mouth. Ryan cracks the knuckles on his right hand. He looks at me, but not at me; I think he's concentrating above me. His eyes refuse to fix.

Do you think breaking and entering is serious?

I didn't break in nothing.

Omar.

We had a key! You saw me go in with a key. How did you not? You said you saw us. You saw us go in with a key. How do you know we weren't invited? You *said* you were watching. You said you saw us go in with a key. I have a MacBook. Do you want it back? I was planning on giving it back—I have it still. I haven't even opened it. It's still in the bag. This is not a big deal—I have everything.

Relax.

How much is a B and E charge?

Kevin stares at me again and licks his lips. He scratches his head and licks lips one more time, wipes his mouth with his hand.

There's a sheen of spit on his hand now. I can see that he has a sharp snaggletooth, with another tooth growing underneath it.

We want you to do something for us.

What?

Don't worry about the house.

Have you arrested Hussain?

No. We don't want to talk to him yet. He punched you—right? Pretty hard? That's the bruise. You are not going to talk to him. We don't want you to. We don't want you going near him.

Can I get a lawyer?

If you get a lawyer, this is over. We hand you over to the police. This—the Reddit posts, the B and E—you are up for all of it. Talking is done.

How do I not get a lawyer?

You want a lawyer? Then there's no bargaining.

Bargaining for what?

We need help with a small thing, then it will be over. We can forget stuff. We need a small thing. Do you remember this? Kevin slides over a small printout, another Reddit post that I wrote right after Anna died. I barely have any idea. Do you still feel like this?

Sure.

It's pretty detailed.

Man, you guys need to calm down. I was joking. Joking. This is a joke. I look at the post. This one isn't even bad.

You can either be in a lot of trouble or no trouble.

I'm not—

There is no middle ground, do you understand? Two officers

saw you breaking and entering into a house. We have a complaint from the inhabitants. Do you understand the severity of that?

I didn't do anything.

Omar, fuck.

What!

Ryan: You are fucking this up! You are fucking your life up! You stupid kid.

Kevin: Ryan. Omar, please listen to us.

This seems weird.

You've put yourself in a bad situation.

I don't know—

You are not grabbing on to anything we are saying to you. Try to understand. Take a deep breath. Understand what we are saying, okay? You have broken the law, but, you know, if you help us, then we know you are of good character, and we can smooth things out.

You want the MacBook back? It's there—it's there in my room. We can zip back and get it.

I want you to go to a mosque for us.

What?

At Bloor and Dufferin. There's a mosque.

You want me to what? Start praying? What?

We want you to go to the mosque and take a look at what happens inside.

People pray, man. What the fuck you think happens? What do you mean you want me to look inside?

Ryan: You need to watch your temper.

Why are you telling me to go to a mosque? You know they do

the thing in Arabic right? That's not a language I speak. There's black dudes in that mosque—I think that's a black mosque. What the fuck am I going to do in there?

South Asians, like you, go in there.

South Asians? Homie, I've been here since I was nine. What the fuck am I going to do about South Asians?

Go inside. It's simple. Go inside. There is someone inside that we're interested in. First, let's keep it simple, go inside, pray, talk to some people.

This is creepy shit.

We know that you care about this country. We're willing to believe that the stuff you said was a joke. We can believe that it was a joke. We are *willing* to understand that it was a joke—

Of course it was a joke. It was me talking on the internet. Who the fuck posts about shit like cutting off people's heads on the internet and then goes and does some actual foolish shit?

We are willing to understand that it was a joke, but if you want us to believe that you're not serious, and that the B and E was a misjudgment, and that you're not an Islamist, a person who wants to derail trains and blow up Bay Street, and you are not threatening our country, then you have to do this.

Y'all are fucking dumb. I feel the same pounce of anger that I had with Harley, in the kitchen, but there the thought of Anna's sadness dampened it. I have to learn to use that sadness, instead, to fling forward. What am I supposed to do?

You go. You go and pray. You listen, you talk. You talk, and you see what they're saying and understand. That's it. Do you speak Hindi?

A bit. Like. A bit. Not a lot.

So you listen. You don't direct the conversation. Go in easy. And you remember everything. That's it. Simple.

How many times am I supposed to do this?

One step at a time, Omar. Day by day. You need to help us. Once you've helped us, then you're done. That's it. It's not hard—it's this little thing. Listening. Praying. Paying attention. Remember the exact—

Are you going to wire me up?

Omar. This is simple. You go in and listen. Don't stress out. Okay? Day by day. Stop thinking about when it's over or whether you'll be wired or this and that. Think about what you're doing.

This is insane.

Omar. What are you going to do?

I don't know.

Deep breath. This is not a bad thing. This is good. This is helping. You're being good. Productive. Do you get that? What are you going to do?

Nothing.

Omar.

I want to get out of there. I repeat after them: Go to a mosque and listen.

Easy. That's it. Go to a mosque and listen.

When they drop me off at home, I don't sleep—but, finally, it's not fear. My anger is shifting to something more useful. I'm excited.

Kevin calls fast the next day, but I ignore it. He leaves a message, after I end up ignoring him all day. My body is not sure yesterday actually happened the way it did. I listen to his message and it's the same as what he said yesterday. He reminds me that this is in my best interest. He reminds me that I want to do this, and it's the easiest path out for me—that it's *the* path for me. How simply did he put it? Like it's a new day job, simple as plating a dish of bloody meat. There's something in me that wants to get carried away with this new momentum, even as I think I can recognize this is a bad way out of a few problems. I can close one wound with this solution, but how many more will it open?

Matthew texts and wants to meet at the Communist's Daughter to check in on me after last night. I want to ignore him, but there's uneasiness in me. The excitement kept me wide-eyed all night. I walk down Spadina, past the dim sum restaurants, and west on Dundas towards him.

He has a new toque that he thinks hides his bald spot that he thinks he's discovered. He won't let me check. It's the receding hairline you have to worry about, I say. He won't talk about Sylvia, keeps licking his fingers. His legs cross over one and then the other and then again, and his sentences are slow and steady and not rat-tat-tat-tat like usual. He licks his fingers again. He has beer foam on his lip and I know that I love him when I move my hand across and wipe it off for him.

I have a small square block of weed someone left on my kitchen counter. It's wrapped in Saran wrap and then aluminum foil.

That's obviously your roommate's, Matthew says.

It's small enough to go missing in a general sweep of a kitchen countertop. Maybe I shouldn't have this on me—what if I get scooped by the RCMP again? The weed has already been pruned, ground, and squished into a hot square, as if it was in someone's back pocket: it has the heat from the shape of an ass.

Matthew tells me this is his favourite bar now, but he keeps shifting in his seat. This is a big deal for him, finding a new bar, not sticking to the old university-era hangouts. He thinks he's growing up. Hanging out at white spots is growing up. The bald spot is freaking him out. Matthew knows what to do with life: he says things before they are true and makes them true.

I start crumbling the weed out of its box fart shape on the table out of the eyeline of the bartender. We are seated near the window; people wait for the streetcar right outside.

You gotta shake out of this.

Out of what?

You can't be sad forever?

She's barely been dead.

You've been ... I know. I know. But you have to be healthy about it.

This is the first joint I've smoked in a while. I think it'll help me fall asleep.

We smoked weed two days ago.

I need help sleeping.

How's Kali?

I don't remember.

It sounds cool. Like what you need.

You know she has a boyfriend?

Some next man in Korea.

They're engaged.

Since when?

She told me.

Sylvia was saying they were kinda breaking up.

Guess not.

Guess not.

Matthew wipes more foam from his mouth. At seven in the evening, after so many beers, it begins to feel like morning in me. He's right, or he's not wrong—I have to crack past my self, my grief. I have to form a life like he does and pretend things do not matter. Is becoming an informer God's way of tagging me in to life? The walls of the bar are yellow, or is it the light? Matthew looks at the bartender and out the window. At the table next to us. He won't look at me.

I can't stop thinking of her dying. Or, of me dying—of getting hit by a car. Getting hit by a car when I cross the street.

Is it someone else that kills you? Matthew looks up and down the bar as he says this. He's shaking his leg.

I'm not going to kill myself.

You're freaking me out.

I'm not going to do anything to myself, I promise. Cross my heart, hope to die.

I saw Sylvia this morning.

How is she? How are you guys?

You're freaking her out.

How?

What were you doing a couple of days ago?

When?

At like three a.m.

Nothing.

She thinks she saw you on College Street, bugged out.

I dunno. Yo, do you think Anna planned it?

Of course she planned it.

She had a prescription for the benzos. Maybe it was an accident.

She gave away her clothes.

So?

So that's a thing. Giving away your shit.

Who'd she give them to?

Emina. She called and asked me if I had a girlfriend or a girl or whoever that I wanted to give the clothes to.

When was this?

Like a week before.

Did you see her?

I went over.

How was she?

Fine.

How fine? She died the next week.

She was Anna, man. Fine. A little bit depressing, but funny. You know, Anna. She was normal. The place looked fine.

How come I didn't know?

It's not an easy thing to know ...

We had broken up six months before. How could I not have known at all?

She was like that. Private.

Yo, I knew the girl for, like, ten years.

Her parents didn't know either.

Fuck that. Fuck them.

They tried with her, you know.

Who tried?

I don't know. It's not like they abandoned her.

I should have felt something.

You can't see that type of thing. The person doesn't want you to.

That's why we broke up.

I haven't spoken yet about the breakup, not really, to Matthew. These six months after we broke up, I kept to myself, like a numb vulture somehow circling its own carcass.

Did she leave you a note?

Bro—

She planned it and didn't leave a note? Come on, yo. How can you die and not want to say a few things? You don't disappear yourself without having a few things to say.

I read once—

You read?

I read once, you know, you're not supposed to find an answer for anything.

What the fuck does that mean?

I think it means to chill.

Yo, a note. A note. A note for me. For real? No note for me? Not an email? Not a Facebook status? Give me a fucking break.

The only thing I have to turn to is my anger and my anger is not even mitigating my pain. I can't be mad at her for not leaving me a note: I can't even conceive of it.

There's a note for me. There has to be.

The callousness of her parents and their constant fuck-ups with her, hiding the note, the meander of her friends—it all makes more sense than no note. I can't organize myself to believe that

I meant nothing to her—that is impossible. I want my anger out of me and into her.

Instead, grief: the blue colour of the flame. Its hottest part.

How long you been wearing that shirt for?

Can you smell me?

You gotta change the shirt.

Anna loved this shirt. I smell my armpits hard in the bathroom. I'm looking for her in that musk. When she lay in bed with me and turned over to face me. The way we spent the day slow, small kisses, our smells warping into each other. I can't find her in that smell.

When I come back, I tell Matthew that I don't even know if I like Anna. I hope for him to look at me with empathy and concern, but instead, he thinks that I've misspoken.

You mean Kali.

I don't want to, but I correct him: Anna.

Matthew does not say anything. The only thing I have to show how important she was to me is duration. I have no keepsakes from our time together.

Then: Do you mean because she killed herself?

No. I say it without knowing if I mean it but knowing that I want to say it and witness what it does to him.

Matthew nods a little bob.

A burst of lightning outside, and for a second, we are both lit up white. Anna throwing them down from heaven not too happy. Did Anna have any childhood friends? I know the answer. She was not like us, immigrants carved from their past by movement. Me and Matthew exactly once talked about what it would be like if we had grown up back home together, but we did not get nostalgic for lost childhood friends: they were figments of imagination. For any real purpose, they did not exist.

She had no past. Anna had refused to see anyone from before fourteen. She said little about them, except to tell me that she would not say anything: life before fourteen did not matter. I knew she was raised in Barrie, or Whitby, or some other white place, and they left because her brother had too many dark friends who were getting in trouble with him. Her father was from North York originally. Their move was treated as a homecoming. I knew when she was twelve some friends had robbed her on Halloween by inviting her over and then mugging her once she entered the front door. Not even of her candy—of her cash. They had punched her in the stomach, and also stolen pieces of her Ninja Turtles outfit. She said she went home crying to her mom, and the distress was deepened because she couldn't go back out. Her costume was ruined. She tried to talk about it in a light tone, but I could hear her voice waver. I didn't know if there were any happy memories or more bad ones.

Matthew is not looking at me. When I asked her about it a few days later she looked at me like I was an idiot. I asked her again and she said: I forget. I told you that? Forgetting is a tool that only some people understand. Matthew looks out the window, his index finger chattering on the table surface, his leg pumping up and down; the nerves are falling out of him and into me, making me nervous.

What's wrong?

I have to talk to you.

We talking.

I gotta talk to you.

What's wrong?

I saw Bernie yesterday. Matthew stops looking out the window and looks at me, but he can't hold the eye contact. He looks out the window, again, at a passing streetcar that stops and opens its doors. No one gets off; a few people get on. Will it snow tonight, later? The bar door opens and shuts quickly and a bark of wind chills us. He gave me a note.

So? About what?

Like. A note.

What it say?

From Anna.

Fuck you.

Bro. Matthew looks back at me. My body freezes; it blows up from inside my stomach, up my chest, like vomit, and expands into my entire body. It cripples me—I cannot move and I stare at Matthew while he breaks eye contact again. My hand is cool on the beer glass, and then it is not, it's hot, and I have to let go, and I put my hand in my pocket to hide the fist I'm making. Do I scream, hit, or sit here dully? Matthew's eyes glow with tears. The tears don't drop, and he wipes them away. He curls his shoulders into himself and is silent. Do you want the note?

Do you have it?

It's at home.

I don't know.

It doesn't say much—

Don't tell me.

Sorry.

No, tell me. Tell me.

It says sorry. It's short. She thanked me.

For what?

Nothing special ... just whatever.

My heart isn't pounding. It is slowing down. Wheezing, barely there. I knew Bernie liked him, because Matthew always had a dark girlfriend, and so Bernie thought he wasn't going to try and fuck his daughter. This isn't Matthew's fault. I don't know. Maybe it is. I have to leave Matthew because I don't know what to do, or what I could do. I look around the bar for something I can use as a weapon. I look for something that will puncture his skin and make all that blood come loose from his body. I don't think I've ever been angry at him and my body is confused. I want to choke him and hold him at the same time. I stare at him, unable to say what I need to, and he looks out the window, allowing the silence to become thick with physicality. I wish, for half a second, that he could get angry at me, and do something about it, so I could stop thinking for a minute. I imagine a future girlfriend asking about my past and looking at the internet for a trail, discovering that my longest girlfriend killed herself. Across from Matthew, I lick the yellow glue on the paper and close the joint. I take the table candle outside and light it, inhale a gulp, let my eyes drop when the smoke sinks into my skull.

How close was Matthew to Anna, exactly? Before I can contain my thoughts they start sliding in a slippery chain—why did he feel so deeply when she died, anyway? Why did he pull himself out from my life so quick when she died? I want to crumble or cry or something as the streetcar makes its way up Spadina. When me and Anna broke up I guessed Matthew would have to choose friendships;, I mean, he had known her for as long as I had, and they would talk too, they went way back, he would talk to her about his girls. I remember them together in the summer, at Dance Cave, dancing while I swayed at the side, too faded from drink, his hands on her hips and the way she moved comfortable with him: I was proud of myself for being so fine with that. They had known each other for ten years. Same as me, same as me. It was so hot in there that night, with so many people, and I never brought it up because I didn't know what I had seen. I had seen nothing, no, not really. Their bodies close, the aura of familiarity, friendship, both moving basically on beat. The way his hands stayed on her hips, the muscles in them, the tendons; finally, when he moved his hands away from her hips, they stayed together while one song phased into another. He leaned into her ear and spoke—she didn't tell me what he said.

The next night, in her bedroom, I wanted to ask her while she rolled a joint, but I was hungover, it was late. I never asked Matthew. She seemed so comfortable with his body, his aggression, the way he moved in unison with her. Maybe it was the booze. We would go to the pool together that summer, before that night, and they would play together in the water, their bodies becoming slowly and slowly familiar. I never questioned it. I liked having a best friend that I didn't question—I liked having two best friends. I would tell Anna again and again that she was my best friend without stopping to think about it.

Once, after the pool, after a blazed day, and her skin red, her soaked bikini on the ground, she started kissing me, and she asked me if I was bored with her.

What do you mean?

We've been together for so long.

I said no, I said no, never, and she said, Not even after all these years? She was wet and tired and sun-drunk. Did we have anything to drink that day? We tried for a beer on a patio, but it was useless; the beer was too heavy and the sun was hanging low and angry, smog everywhere in the daytime. She laughed and asked me if it would be fun to bring someone into bed and I said no. Then I said who? And I asked her who she wanted to fuck, and she said, Anybody, nobody, it doesn't matter, I'm joking, and she kissed me on the lips and I asked her, maybe I was drunk, I don't think so, I asked her if she wanted to fuck Matthew and she said, What! And we had this normal conversation while I slid into her, still half-hard, but filling up, and she was wet, and she said she didn't say that, that's not what she meant, but her head moved back and she let me kiss her on the neck, a thing she generally didn't allow (she was afraid of marks), and didn't ask me to stop and I asked her to think of Matthew fucking her with me and as quickly as I started she must have been drunk because she told me to cum in her and she asked for it again and again, which I was so unused to and she clenched onto me and started asking for me to *please* do it and I came and I lay on top of her after and stayed in her, which she did not allow; usually by now she would be rushing to squat over the toilet and watch my sperm drop out. I don't know how long it had been or how loud we had been, but we lay there and didn't say anything. We didn't fuck for a month after that—I saw her once a week, we talked almost every day, said good night in texts, but her body went away from me.

A raccoon comes down the side of the building, fat boy clanking on a metal ladder I can't see. The moon is big and hot tonight, beaming like the white eye of God. The raccoon's wobble stops. He looks at me, his belly just above the ground, aluminum foil flecked in his mouth. I'm outside our old apartment building at Yonge and Eglinton. Tender brown and yellow bricks, and when I look up at the topmost windows, our old apartment on the fourth floor, I see the same wide-open windows to let the heat out. It's an old building and when the first, second, third floors turn their heat up, it rises to suffocate the fourth floor, even in the winter. The windows have to stay open. When it snows outside, it boils inside.

Bernie owns this building. It is old and rotten. The first four months me and Anna lived here I did not know that it was a family-owned thing. I gave her $650 on the fourth of every month in cash, and she paid the person she called our landlord. He was our landlord, correct—she lived in this kind of slippery crevice of language. I came home early one day and the two of them were in our kitchen, whisper-fighting, a pot of tea cooling on our breakfast table. The rain was hammering outside and towels were stopping a leak near our window. I remember his yellow teeth matched his zip-up sweater. I'm scared of rich people who don't fix their teeth. Rich people who can't accept their wealth.

Bernie: Oh ... I didn't know Anna had guests ...

I looked at the key in my hand, and Anna left the kitchen without speaking and stuck her head out the window, pretending to source our leak. I didn't say anything to Bernie, reminded Anna that the leak was going to create more water damage, and shut myself in our bedroom. This was my house and that was my right. Our shoulders must have touched as I made my way past him.

You didn't even tell him to take his shoes off? I said to her later.

I had slippers for guests that cost me twenty dollars. She was gasping for air. She reverted to this panic attack in moments like this, and I knew that they could be fake, the way they activated the moment she needed them to, to get away from me.

I'm still on his health insurance. He had to drop something off. He owns the building.

The walls of our apartment began sweating with this revelation. Her head was still outside the window and she took in big chunks of piercing air. I grabbed her by the belt and pulled her in. She sat silent. All this would be hers someday: my rent was going towards a mortgage that, on his death, would be given to her. I don't know how many other properties they owned, but even one building in midtown Toronto had to make them millionaires, on paper, even if Bernie was the type to claim his "liquid cash" was tight. When she sat quiet my anger surprised me by moving on.

At least now I'll marry rich, I joked.

I didn't think to ask what medication Bernie was bringing her. I knew of at least three pills that her doctor was trying in combination. She had emergency benzos. She had a daily pill. She had an evening one, for sleep. She could disappear into the bathroom and reappear a different person. I wondered what Anna would be like if the doctor managed to extinguish the flame that was scorching her, but I didn't think I had the capacity to enquire. I hope the note she left me revealed it all in detail.

Outside the building now, the memory of her as violent as anything real, I remember going through the prescription bottles in the bathroom, the long science names making me feel ESL again. They were like spells and if I could pronounce them accurate they would reveal something about her.

I didn't feel guilt when I eyed those bottles and their long names. She had left me out of the decision, just telling me that her sex drive would bounce up and down. Instead, a coalition of family and Emina and others persuaded her to see a psychologist. When I touched the orange plastic bottles, I wondered what they did, what power they held over her, but I didn't ask. I realized I had not signed a lease, and none of the furniture in this apartment, except a dresser, was mine. The pills seemed to work: she slept regularly. The one side effect she complained about was night sweats.

Did she stop taking them? I don't know. Again, I didn't ask—I wanted the medication to quiet down what was raging in her, because it meant she would have enough energy left to soothe me. If she began a new medication, I knew, because she became sleepy for a month, taking two-to-three-hour naps in the middle of the day. Her day would be divided in half by these. She would be sound asleep when I left for work at three p.m. and startling awake at two a.m. when I got back. She would ask me to cook for her, and it was enough if I pan-fried some dumplings. After the last new pill, when I still lived with her, and her sleeping schedule came back to normal, I finally asked if they were working. Anna grabbed my cheek with her hand and then clutched my chin. It began to hurt.

Of course they are.

I moved out for the last time two months later. I packed three pairs of Nikes, a duffle bag full of clothes, and that was it. I left in the afternoon, while she was in class, and felt no urge to leave an explanation. She would understand. I texted Emina to let her know what I was doing but was too scared to outright admit that me and Anna had not spoken about it.

Her parents' house is long and narrow, two windows up top, two windows on the main floor, and a tiny crack of chimney on the right side. A kid's drawing. A puff of smoke. Their lawn is brown-green and cut badly, short near the roadside but tufted near the windows. One-car drive with a black Lexus that I squeeze past. The wooden gate to the back has no clasp; it swings lightly. The side window over the kitchen seems like a good entry point: the motion detector light near the side door comes on. I wait. My breath in the air, and I'm sure there's a raccoon somewhere I can't see. No shadows, no movements. I move again.

The kitchen window looks large enough to fit me. I look around for something to stand on. The light has gone off, but when I move, it pops back on. I convince myself that nothing will happen. It's okay. It's cool. I flip over the empty recycling box and look at the window. A small wooden block in place to prevent it from being opened. It has not been slotted correctly, and with a little nudge

I could move it, but it'll fall into the sink and make a noise that will travel upstairs.

I watched a few YouTube videos on lock-picking. I don't want to break the window or cut the mesh: I want to be a ghost, to visit Anna like she is. There are no cars on the street. It doesn't matter. I look to the sky and ask who's watching. I've been to this house a few times before and a small memory tumbles at me. It was an awkward dinner, a birthday party, I think seventeen, and she introduced me to her parents as her friend. We had emailed about this—I was warned—but a shot of pain came at me anyway. Her parents allowed us to drink beer in the basement (only beer, no hard liquor), and I swallowed five straight. She drank nine and puked, evergreen. I held her hair over the toilet until Bernie came down and asked me to leave. Her hair was matted to her skull-skin by all the hot sweat that appears when a body moves with sickness. I held her nape when she puked, and even then I wanted to kiss her. I wanted her father to see that—to know I wanted to fuck his daughter; I didn't want to hide anything, I wanted that revenge of desire, for him to know that I had fucked her.

The YouTube videos are gone from my memory. Too long and complicated for my nerves. I have no idea how to pick a lock. My brain tried to pay attention, but I didn't have the small tool you need, and instead, I snake a small screwdriver from Nathan's tool box into the keyhole. I wrote down these notes on how to pick a lock on my phone, but the light hurts in the pitch black. A raccoon moves big in the backyard. I do remember the diagram of the lock, the pistons inside the metal case moving up or down depending on how you twisted the tiny criminal rod. I kneel in front of the door and blast cellphone light. I wiggle the screwdriver: nothing. I twist and hope for something, but the lock does not indulge. Allah, please, I ask, but he's not interested. He's up there sipping martinis with Anna.

I move back. I should give this up. I can't sneak into this house without a trace. I am not a ghost. I am not a ghost. I promise I am not a ghost.

In front of the Lexus is a long basement window. It is thin and stretches half the length of the house from where I remember stairs lead to the bathroom. This window is slotted crooked into its grooves. I contain myself and don't smash it. I cut the mesh out. I apply pressure, more and more, like squeezing a head, and the glass pops gently, deep cracks appearing on its surface. With a push, I take the biggest piece of glass out and then remove the others. The metal frame singes my skin in the cold. I wish there was something I could do about my skin, that there was a prayer I could say to turn into metal and gold and strong. My heart pumps for me. It doesn't matter. I pop my head in, but there's a drop to the ground, so I go in feet first and land on my heels. The pain goes all the way into my back.

I wait to adjust to the black.

I make my way towards the stairs.

The basement is barely furnished—concrete uncovered everywhere, a few pieces of furniture in zigzagged order, and there's one plugged-in freezer and one unplugged freezer. Next to the staircase, fibreglass insulation bleeds out. The wood is unfinished. It's the meanest basement I've been in. I don't remember it being like this; I remember a couch, a TV, the soft light on kids drinking.

That night, I held her palm for a minute and she was moist with sweat. She hated how much she would sweat on her upper lip.

I creak onto the main floor. I count to thirty and examine my breath: one, two, one two, one two three four five. No one is coming. This will only work with patience and calm.

The main floor has small lights: nightlight, microwave, phone, the red eye of the TV. I know her bedroom is next to the parents' office on the second floor. I don't know which is which, though. The third floor has a bathroom and the master bedroom.

Up the stairs quiet is easy. I have to guess which door is hers; both are ajar and there are beds in both rooms, but I can see a man's foot on the bed through the door on the left. The foot turns and I know it's her father by the movement she picked up from him. She had restless legs and would sweat the bed wet. Her father twists his ankle and it cracks and pops. I stand still. The noise moves through the house like an animal would, and he twitches and murmurs like she would. She said these little quakes were a product of her medication, some antidepressant, but here it is in her father. Unless it's her ghost inhabiting him. I hope he isn't sleeping in her bed. I move to the empty room and it's been cleaned out like a guest bedroom, but it is hers. They've moved back everything, all her books and belongings, pens, notebooks. Posters on the wall—Hanson, Korn, Linkin Park. An arc of childhood taste. I'm caught by a savage hunger so good that I stop on the bed and breathe. When was the last time I ate? I remember a little tube of Pringles.

In our apartment, she would look at me from underneath the bedsheets, her bottom half covered, her breasts bare, her journal in her hand. She would ask me not to look at her diary. I never did—I remember once she left it on the bed and I stared at it for five minutes, breathing it in. It had a black card stock cover. I opened it and read the inscription, her full name, the year, how much of a reward she would give if it was returned—twenty bucks. I closed it and let it lie on the bed.

She moved out from her parents' house, she said, to collect herself, to pull it together. She wanted to go to Montreal, Vancouver, or she had heard about a resort off Nova Scotia or New Brunswick with a hotel that you could work in and never run into anyone you know and save money and sit on that cash like a king. I can feel her imprint in the room. Her diaries would be in the closet. Or they might be with her parents, who might be poring over them for their own forensic work. Would they read them? It would maybe be too soon to learn her thoughts. Could I ask her parents to let me move in with them, to take care of me?

The bedsheets are tucked into the corners and the room's been recently dusted. The closet door is open and her clothes are carefully hung or folded. They've made it seem like she's gone on vacation. The only real indication of Anna's absence—aside from the cleanliness—is the boxes. Two large boxes and about five smaller ones, and three shoeboxes. I look at her bookshelf and there are a dozen university textbooks from her poli sci courses. My instinct is to curl into the bed and fall asleep, but I'm terrified of the bed. What if her ghost is here? What if her mother comes in every morning and sniffs the pillowcase, what if she's preserving that tinge of Anna and I'm ruining it now with my own scent? There's a small bowl of potpourri on the desk by the window. Her computer is shut down.

On the desk there's a small Vans shoebox, black, frayed. Maybe she hid a note for me to find—she knew what I was capable of, always, before I did; she would always ask me if I was upset when I was in the middle of a silent tantrum, aware of my anger before I could articulate it. I open it. It's full of papers. I have to breathe and part the blinds. I stare at the street light—white—until my eyes hurt, and I look back at the box. There's a red pen. She went over my high-school homework, college essays. A red ink Japanese pen, the same brand she used to correct the same spelling mistakes over the years: *definitley,* I could never spell. A blue pen: she would draw on my back with blue ink. Zeppelins, aeroplanes, zebras, as the slow cherry of a joint would fade. It would hit me hard: I would already be asleep, and for ten minutes she would doodle before finding something to watch on TV. This box is a little clusterfuck of memories. Love notes from high school, from university, a scatter of photographs that I printed out for her twenty-first birthday. It's not so long ago that we were in love, and then suddenly, the door shut. With this box open, and these memories, I try to read the narrative she made for us. Is this how I could get to know her—by seeing how she knew us? The photos stop at twenty-five, when we had our most serious rupture, when on/off became mostly off. There's a photo of her and Emina at Emina's graduation. Anna is holding a bouquet of sunflowers, smiles spilled wild on their faces. The old campus buildings are in the background. They're about to break into laughter. There is a smaller brown box inside this one that says *Peoples Jewellers.*

I don't think I bought her anything from there. I take the lid off and there is a small collection of notes, not in my handwriting, a few TTC transfers. A stack of eight photo booth photographs: her and Owen. She looks happy; he is lean, slouched, comfortable: he's not confused about his place in her life. I dig through the Vans box and there is another smaller box, with handwriting I don't recognize. Two essays from university with Bs. This isn't a box of me and her—this is a box of years, the accumulation of her life. This is a box of her life, not our life. There is no box just for us.

There is a photo of Anna and Owen taken in this house, at the table, with a cake, a small birthday cake, and her mother off to the side. I can't tell how old she is—but there is Owen. This must be twenty-five. Two years ago. Her father would have taken this. Again: happiness that is calm, secure, steady, moving like a stream in a forest. Something I couldn't provide, that she couldn't find with me.

I'm startled to realize now, so late, that I didn't know her, that a photo like this could catch my surprise. I remember her twenty-fourth birthday and the happiness that invaded our little apartment and how buoyed she was by calmness. We did not fight for almost a month, and I thought it was because of me and my exhaustion at our fighting—the fights belonged to me, I was the one with the temper, but I was exhausted from work, with her, and I thought we weren't fighting because I couldn't do it anymore. The way she moved around the apartment, slowly, moving the vase, asking me if I could help move the couch; I thought we had moved into another epoch. Anna on the couch, the buttons of her white shirt open, her arm outstretched, her hand open, her index pointing to the remote. Our first couch, our first apartment. When we broke apart for the last time that month, it was for good. I wasn't allowed to possess her anymore, she said, but I did, in secret; I expected something in return always.

Are you out of your fucking mind? Her father runs into the room.

No.

What the fuck are you doing?

The smaller box drops out of my hand into the larger box. It makes no noise, or I can't hear it—my senses pick him up in his robe and belly and thin line of hair up to his chest. His cheeks are red. I've never seen anyone his age in their pajamas.

How did you get in?

Through the front door. The door was open.

The door is locked.

It was open.

Did you break into my house?

I came in.

He doesn't exactly know what to do with his anger. I imagine the room blowing up, a Coke bottle exploding after being shook. Bernie stands dead still. So still, except his mouth and fluttering lips. His fat tongue making a sound at me, mostly the same thing over and over in different lashes, trying to understand.

You broke into my house.

No.

No?!

No—I wanted to see.

How did you—

The door was open.

It wasn't.

There's a note for me, from her.

Omar, I don't know who you think you are.

She would have left me a note.

Omar, please. We told you—

You called me after she died.

Did you live with her?

Don't play stupid.

She was not well.

Oh, fuck off.

Her mother—

Bernie. Did she leave anything for me?

She didn't.

She left a note for me.

She left a note for me and her mother.

She left me a note.

Omar. She left a few notes. She didn't for you. One for me, for Emina, you know Emina, for her mother, for that boy Owen, her ex—

What!

I've called the police. Omar, don't move, please. I've called the police.

Her mother appears in the background, with an eight-inch chef's knife dangling from her hand. She is holding it carelessly, like a set of keys. She came to save me from Bernie—her shoulders are Anna's. We could share a cup of wine downstairs with the police officers. Blue and red lights blaring in the background.

Her hair looks like a knot Anna would brush out. Bernie looks in pain, as if for a moment, she did stab him.

There are worse things I could be doing here, I tell them. I could be here for bad reasons! I'm here for the note. I could be a thief. I could be a murderer. I could be jerking off onto her linens. I was not here to steal anything, I say, but to read. Aren't I owed something? Why was Anna's loss only yours and hers? What if I realized too late that I had lost something? What if I wasn't done knowing Anna—what if I hadn't started?

Her mother loosens her grip on the knife, and it looks as if it'll soon fall to the floor, or be flung at me. Freezing rain outside and small clots of hail punching the ground. I look into Anna's computer screen and wish an animal would pounce out, kill me, or at least knock me out the window and into the wilderness. Behind the computer is a corkboard with photographs of Anna tacked onto it.

Omar.

I don't believe you.

Are you drunk?

Of course not. I'm a Muslim.

I'm sorry—we've already called the police. We didn't know it was you.

The snow arrives after. Anna's parents look at me through the window of the police car. I haven't been cuffed but placed in the back seat. I can't tell what they are talking about. I try to read Bernie's lips—he explains that nothing is to come of this. That I'm harmless.

The cops drive me to the station without a word. I ask them what is happening and they say nothing, take me into a small room and tell me to wait. I sit relaxed in the chair, in the blank room, no posters, no nothing on the walls. A security camera watches me. It feels like at least an hour, or two or three. My blood slows down over however long it is. Even with this new confrontation, I don't believe Bernie. I know I have to keep searching and plunging further down, until I find it.

The door opens. It's Kevin and Ryan, looking like fresh dildos in a display case. They've refreshed the same RCMP buzz cut angled the same way: all sheen and clear skin. They absolutely must keep meticulous records of each other's highest bench press. They ooze in, eager to see me.

My man, Omar.

What you doing here.

You're ignoring my phone calls. I told you that we wanted you to help us.

How am I going to help you?

Another house?

This was different.

We know. We read the officer's notes—you know the family? Kevin opens his arms wide and gestures. Can I make this easy?

You wanna drop me home?

You broke into another house, which is kind of crazy.

It was different.

Two houses! After getting caught already.

They're not pressing charges.

No, they are kind.

What do you want, then?

The cops have stepped back because we've asked them to. We have a lot here to prosecute you with—you want that?

No.

We found another mosque, not a black one—Queen and Lansdowne.

Okay.

We want you to go in and take a look around.

I don't know what to do in a mosque—

Don't you want to do something useful? Kevin begins to try different tactics. He cocks his head and looks at me like I'm making the dumbest choice in the world. Most of my days now, not sleeping, not awake, not with anyone, even when I am—I should be happy to come under Kevin's thumb. I could start to see how much I was missing out on.

I don't answer and Kevin sighs: We pay.

What do you mean you pay?

We pay—it's a job. Treat it like a job.

I thought it was me helping myself out?

You are helping yourself out, and we'll pay.

How much?

I can start with a hundred and twenty-five per day.

For real?

For real.

What do I have to do?

For now? Like I said. Go in. Pray. Talk to the imam. Hang out. Let me know what you see, what they say. Take it easy. Be a good, curious Muslim. I watch Kevin lick his lips. This seems too easy. I wonder if his bosses have promised him something for wrangling me in.

That's it?

That's it.

You pay cash or what?

Yeah, we can pay cash.

I'm late on my rent.

Do this first thing, see how it goes, and then we start talking about more money.

My rent is five hundred a month ...

You're not useful to me at all yet.

I didn't rob anyone—

Omar, stop.

Fine. Fine. Fine!

I have to ask myself again if this is an okay thing to do. My stack of Grappa's cash is small. I look up in case I can catch Anna watching and ask her if this is okay to do.

In elementary school we were shown a picture of a multicultural mosaic. It was a lesson on our civic construction. Everyone seemed to understand, or didn't say anything, but I could never figure out how exactly I was supposed to be part of it. I knew that White was only possible if it had Brown to stand on, but what I was supposed to do under all that weight was not clear. Here, Kevin is offering me a way out, and a way in. His battering conversation is unveiling an appealing idea: to finally join everyone else. Maybe Matthew will be proud—a job offer! Kevin is making it seem as banal as a nine-to-five, but I feel uneasy; I don't want to have to report back on anyone.

Keep your phone on. We'll call soon.

It's twelve, and Kali has gotten off her shift, so I head to hers and bang loony on her door until George opens. He's holding a spatula for protection; maybe I should get them a baseball bat. He reminds me of Mary and her dangling knife ready to filet me open. How did they not have a note for me? I know it should be a dead end—it looks like a pitch-black road to find the thing, but anything could be hidden in that dark.

You scared me, Kali says, peeking from her bedroom door.

Can I come in?

I retrace my steps from the break-in to get to her room. George's door is closed, a brand-new hinge affixed to it with a gigantic brass padlock. I tell myself that it is okay—that I have all of her things, even if I haven't returned them (how do I do that?). It's okay; I'm a ghost, visiting this life—visiting Kali, Matthew, the rest.

She's at the edge of her bed on a pillow, her knees against her breasts. There was, like, this bomb drill in South Korea.

What do you mean?

I don't know. Sock was so ... chill about it. He said it was a normal thing, that the North just threatens them once in a while.

I didn't see anything on the news.

Isn't that weird? That like ... bomb annihilation is day to day.

Sure.

Sure. She rolls her eyes and deepens her voice to mock me. The whole time, I'm standing at the foot of the bed. She is not sending out any sort of vibe I understand. I take my coat off and am about to get on the bed when she tells me to stop.

The cops called. I didn't even realize this, but it wasn't a "break-in." Nothing was broken. No glass. The lock or window or anything. The cops said someone would have known about the key, or looked for it. They asked me who knew about the key.

That's fucked.

No broken glass. It must have been one of George's stupid friends. Okay: come.

She opens her arms and I crawl towards her on the bed and fold into her. She's passive with her body and I take her clothes off, leaving her bra on because she tells me to. When we fuck she clinches her hands on my hips and I know she won't let me change positions. Eventually, kissing seems too much and I bury my head into the pillow until I cum into the condom. She wiggles away and takes a shower, alone. She comes back, dripping.

He's supposed to text me.

What time is it there? I'm sure he will. I don't ask—I grab her as she takes off the towel and reaches for her pajama set.

No, I'm clean.

I kiss her stomach. I'm not horny again, but I hold on to her wet body. She doesn't know what to do, and I feel this enraged energy to not let her go no matter what. I keep kissing her body, not wanting to fuck, but not wanting to let go. Her phone chimes and she tries to move towards it.

Stay? I ask.

Kali looks at her phone: disappointed. You don't have to stay. I'm still naked and unclean, my dick sticky from that weird condom slime. He might call again.

I ask her if she'll hold me and she does for three minutes before her arm falls asleep and she pulls it back—it doesn't matter. She puts her head near my chest and I feel her breath wet-wick my neck and it's good to feel a living breathing person. She doesn't sleep like Anna. Her legs come out from the sheets. Her snoring is gusts, more sporadic, but a full lungful in its strength, a real motor-revving type, a real scare-the-raccoons-away type. Is that all? I look over this barely-known body. It's not even a thing to compare to Anna. She seems less fraught: but for how long have I discovered her? She turns in her sleep and nuzzles against me, breathing against me; her breath is cold and wet on my body and the room is so hot. She was splintered nerves, but I've helped. It's amazing to control both the cause and the comfort. She thanked me three separate times before she came into bed for sleep. She turns and I can see four freckles on her front shoulder and I try to remember what Anna had—but no. Not like that. I cannot graft her onto this lived experience without losing some of her. I press my body into Kali's to try to wake her up for a fuck, but she grumbles without opening her eyes: It's too hot. She thinks I want to cuddle. I press myself against her ass and she repeats herself. I cannot grasp her. I see no shape.

In the morning we walk down to Mars, and she keeps dipping her tiny spoon into her Americano's crema and licking it off. She licks it again and laughs at me. Her scone crumbles in her lap. I tell her I want a cigarette, but she has also quit.

I miss it, she says, and fakes smoking for me. I feel good, though. I ran five K yesterday.

The sun is above us, looking as if it's about to splatter, dark clouds coming across. It reflects off the snowbanks, making it impossible to see straight ahead. I tell her in a short whisper that she has the nicest breasts I've ever seen, anchored by tiny nipples.

She laughs and clutches them for me, and I feel better and ask her why she never wears low-cut dresses, and she flicks away the question, telling me it's none of my business.

I want to know. I ask again.

She wants to be modest, she says, her breasts attract too much attention. It's not modesty, she changes her mind, sipping from her cup, it's trying to control the attention. She looks me right in the eyes when she says this.

The server walks by and I give a food order. Now there is a lank wave of silence between us: Kali looks straight from the menu to the newspaper, back to the menu, and raises her hand to call over and consult the waiter; neither of them make note of me. She moves the spoon to her mouth again and a cord pops in her neck. It looks like a pipe would. I've never noticed it before. She's mostly ignoring me, and I think I'm fine with it, but no, I'm not. Kali takes a hot sip and then slowly adds brown sugar to her coffee. She tilts the spoon sideways and the granules plop into the dark.

What are you doing this weekend?

Nothing really. I think me and—do you mind if I talk about Sock?

Of course not. That was a lie. Desire dosed with rage brewed in me when she said his name; I could feel it prick my heart, anger that was the beginning of love. It wasn't even that my mind thought of them together; it was that it turned her neck into something for me to sink my teeth into.

She goes on: they were going to Skype.

I can't understand the point of a relationship like theirs, but I can read the warm flush of blood rising underneath her skin when she says his name. Even so far away, he seems close to her when she says his name, as if he does exist somewhere in her, as if she had found a tonic for loneliness. It couldn't be true, because I have felt wave after wave of crushing intimacy with her too, but it's easy to get carried away in the thrush of fucking, our tempos aligned, face-to-face, sweating together.

It must be Kali. She can conjure it. She is able to provide a guarded vulnerability that was enough to lull me in but is not what she has with Socrates. That she loved him forcefully I could see in the way her blood rose under skin, threatening to leak. I want to take her back to the apartment and lock us both in the room until she agrees to give me everything she reserves for him; I want to take her to a blackened room until she forgets who is who. She keeps making a face at her coffee, and I pull in the urge to swipe it off the table and onto the floor.

I think we should stop.

I know.

Me and Socrates talked about what we want, after, when we get married—

Does he know?

I told him.

What?

He asked. He's thinking, though, and I think I agree, that you know—going forward.

Sure. I don't know. Sure. Sure, fine.

What are you feeling?

Don't be ridiculous.

Don't be a jerk.

Nothing.

Kali: I care about you.

I am fine. I didn't think you were going to tell him, but yeah.

She dips the spoon again, licks the crema, drops it onto the plate, and sips from the cup. She hasn't washed off last night's makeup or sweat.

Have you talked to anyone about Anna?

What?

Like a therapist?

About what?

About Anna?

About what?

Omar—about Anna. How are you feeling?

Nah ... I don't think this is—I don't think this is necessarily—

I'm your friend.

Okay, sure, but like—

I don't want to push, but if you want to talk about it ... Maybe it's important for you to find someone to express these things to.

Isn't that you?

And, you know—boundaries.

So, not you.

I have trouble with boundaries too.

Is she being real? Is she nervous? I've lost my ability to judge. I cannot see my strength in this situation. I lay my paw across the table and clasp her fingers. She doesn't want me to touch her, but her fingers stay with mine. Short and thin hairs sprout on her knuckles. Her forearm looks like she shaves it. I expect her to be warm, but I'm feeling jagged edges instead. On the walk over I leaned into her body to replicate last night, and I hoped she would pull me in; instead, her body rigid, she pointed at how weird some of the houses in the Annex are.

At home, I open chicken-flavoured Mr. Noodles. I empty the flavour sachet into the packet, twist the opening shut, shake, break the noodles, and eat out of it like a bag of chips while looking out my window. Last night, when I arrived home, I tried to fall asleep to the sound of Nathan violently brushing his teeth. His girlfriend wandered through the hallway this morning, and they had packed bags for Christmas. Where are you from? I thought to ask Nathan, and he said Ottawa, and he said he was going home for a while. Jesus did a tour of India, I told him, and I told his girlfriend. He smokes a lot of weed, I heard Nathan say, by way of explanation. I am glad I am not high right now; I don't have enough money for munchies. How hard would it be to grow weed under this blaring winter sun? The winter sun should be illegal; it's a little trick it plays. My sneakers are still wet from last night. I missed Anna for real this morning, and I missed one thing in particular: the way she teased me at doorways. She would stand still and occupy the entire frame, refusing to let me pass when I was late for work, only when I was late—she loved the trick of frustrating me and making me laugh, knowing that her playfulness would eventually delight me. I'd be late, but a smile would prowl onto my face when I apologized to my chef.

My phone buzzes again and again. I glance at the screen. I didn't save his number, but I recognize Kevin's blaring digits. I thought he would forget me eventually, or that my constant blundering would somehow get him to realize I had no idea what I was doing. My lack of resources or connections in the community means nothing to him. How hard could it be to blend in?

Was I going to do it? His badgering had actually gotten me to evaluate myself, and I couldn't deny the pull of my Reddit posts. There was something alluring about public damage, as shallow as it was. It's amazing that Kevin thinks I would undertake such a massive effort to leave such a petty scar. I hadn't been thinking much when I wrote them, but I knew that in some sense they were true, even if they were ridiculous, but also that they were private, even if on Reddit. How could Kevin not see that? He's trying to seduce me into thinking my words might be actions.

I think about writing a final note to Anna, to balance out the one I haven't found yet.

Five minutes later, Kevin calls again. Could there be a home in informing for me? I search myself for other incidents of tattletaling and can think of no others. I'm too embarrassed to ask Matthew for help, to explain that I'm relying on childhood, still, to make urgent decisions.

The phone is silent. The r/toronto and r/canada sections are quiet. I follow that impulse agitating in me:

> *the toronto 18 were heroes, brothers. and that informer mubin is a coward and race traitor who will hear about it forever. what holds us back? we do! the brothers had a good plan and who held us back? one of our own. it's sad that it's come to this but be wary of what it means*

that we cannot trust our own, how money is turning us on each other.

Kevin had confirmed that posting like this on Reddit was a nonstarter, that I had avoided serious trouble by staying away from actual terrorist networks on Twitter and Facebook; even if he knew about them, I wanted to keep doing them. I felt their power. It didn't matter so much who was reading them but that I was able to post them. I liked being blocked, banned, or having short, one-sentence answers shot at me. I was beginning to understand the strength of frustration and this kind of light delinquency. That it had brought the RCMP into my life was remarkable; it showed me that they were desperate, and because of that, I did have some strength.

think twice, think thrice, about who you trust and how you love. inshallah it is not for everyone.

My neighbours two doors over finished renovating this summer. The house is a modernist rectangle coming out of nowhere in between all these old brownstones, with an Audi in the driveway, and I know the father takes a Benz to work, one of the new SUVs. Their son is visiting for the holidays—a Beemer. I slip on a balaclava and large camo-printed jacket. The sun is crashing hard on the snow. They're Italian—the son's wife fusses with lunch through the window. Last night's snow should be easy to shovel. The driveway looks like at least fifty bucks' worth for two hours.

The snow squeaks under my boots as I walk over, and it would be so much easier to sneak into the house and steal things. Imagine how much me and Hussain could sell a TV for.

Before I knock on the door, I pull my balaclava up over my face and smile. The smile starts to come undone, but I hold it and I feel like I might cry if I keep fake smiling, so I drop it and knock on the door. I don't think I look like a threat—only grubby. The woman opens the door full of nerves and the baby in her arms.

Do you need shovelling? I ask, and she closes the door after smiling and saying yes. She locks the door. When she opens the door again, the baby is gone and she is wearing a hard grimace.

For twenty dollars?

It's a big driveway. I do it for fifty, usually.

You've shovelled this before?

Driveways this size.

I have thirty cash on me.

Do you want to pull the Audi in?

It takes no time for my elbows to start hurting. My triceps. Grandfather comes out and watches and shifts in his jacket. He lights a cigarette, watches me, doesn't speak. Maybe they're Portuguese. He looks like slow-cooked meat, like the flesh would slide off his face with ease. He takes about two pulls to finish the smoke and goes in. I'm having an out-of-body drone cam experience where I can see myself in this ridiculous teenage situation, shovelling snow for money. While my muscles heat up, I get light-headed. The sun bouncing off the snow doesn't help. It feels as if I'm watching myself complete these movements on a TV.

Before Kevin, I had not spoken to a cop in three years. The

last time I had been walking late at night with Anna and it was dark, like night was going to take over forever. We were a little drunk, three gin and tonics each, and the cop car curled around a corner and slowed next to us. Anna kept walking. I stopped, then followed. The window rolled down and it was too cold for it. The driver was white and the partner a Chinese guy, both with movie-cop crew cuts. Their bulletproof vests so bulky they could not really twist, had to turn their entire bodies. They looked at Anna long. She was fully covered up, but they still bore their vision on her, trying to X-ray through all the bulky winter gear. Her $500 coyote-trim parka. Her red face was uncovered except for its winter glow and booze blush, and her sniffling all that snot back. Her face was as bright as these snowbanks. The cop's eyes finished gobbling her up, and then turned to me. They asked Anna if she was okay. Nice guys. She said yes. Yes, of course. They didn't speak to me. They rolled their window back up and drove off towards our home but stopped at a red light. I swear they were looking back at me. We followed hand in hand, until I lost my nerve and had to stand inside a 7-Eleven, taking swigs of hot dog air until I was calm.

I'm halfway through the driveway and ready to turn off. This Mr. Noodle diet isn't giving me enough fuel to shovel this driveway. The wife is looking at me with her baby from the window, and I'm embarrassed to be slowing down already. I could live in a castle of Mr. Noodles with Kevin's offer of $125 a day.

When I told Anna I did not want to live in Bernie's building, her response was Why don't we work at his dealership? I was stunned and did not say anything, but I knew this could be a way out. I liked the idea of working at a car dealership, and for a week, I pretended cars were my hobby. I looked at Nissan engines online and studied the different models. I looked at photographs of the metal husks and watched YouTube videos on the intricacies of engine performance. I wanted to be prepared for an off-the-cuff phone call.

Anna had stopped attending classes. Bernie gave her an admin assistant position and she lasted one winter, even though she did nothing all day/there was nothing to do. She said a salesman didn't need a degree. I had not thought of this. I did not think I could sell a single thing, but I knew I could make it at least three months—the winter—without getting fired, maybe four if Bernie took pity on me. If I saved those cheques, I could manage at least the summer without worrying much about a job.

The offer never came. When I asked, she said, Recession. She shrugged. It gave me a sense of how different tribes operate when a boot presses down; of course Bernie would protect his lifestyle before our relationship. I felt no anger when she shrugged.

I look at the missed call from Kevin on my phone: $125 a day.

I'm at the Coffee Time at Queen and Lansdowne, lingering, sipping. I burned my tongue in the beginning, so it almost doesn't matter what anything tastes like. I have a chocolate dip donut. I watch the mosque—I'm worried because I'm going to stick out. I text Kevin and say that a lot of black people are going in, and he tells me not to worry about anything, that it's a Pakistani mosque, and I say I'm not Pakistani, and he says not to worry, again. He tells me not to worry over and over. I tell him that I think it's a

Somali mosque and I should not be doing this, that they will spot me easy quick. This is where he gets upset and tells me that he doesn't care and that I have to go in and talk to people. He says these are his instructions: go in, talk to people, be honest, be friendly. That's it. I ask him what the point of that is, and he says that they have a larger point, but they don't want to overwhelm me. He thinks I am stupid and incapable, or there is no trust.

I finish a second coffee and toss the paper cup. I look through the window onto Queen and pause; I can see myself in the glass and a streetcar moves through my reflection. I am wearing my last clean button-down shirt, a blue oxford, and I flatten it against my body and brush my hair back. My jeans are clean. My Nikes have small scuffs on them, but I can't do anything about that.

I cross the street slowly, not waiting for the light to turn, walk towards the mosque, and let an old man with a long beard enter before me. His son follows him, wearing a salwar kameez and Jordans—his beard is long too, but sculpted, the hair ending in a pristine line above his lip, his cheeks freshly shorn, and I peek a gold chain on his neck. We look each other in the eyes and he won't break contact and he moves past me and I let him, a cheap aggression looping off his body that dissolves once he disappears into the building.

The building is like a barn. Shoes are cluttered against each other at the entrance. The air is hot with the smell of tobacco. I don't know what to do. It's been ages since I've been in a mosque, and even then, I followed my father's lead; when we got inside for prayer, lined up in rows, he told me to follow what everyone else did. What's important is the prostrations and the community, the way your body bends towards Mecca in neat lines pointed east. I remember the way the Arabic came out from a loudspeaker, or was it the imam? I remember the length of the language and how all the men's bodies moved up and down together, eyelids fluttering or closed, all towards the Kaaba, all asking for the same thing, all giving our secrets to Him.

The carpet is green and old, clean and well maintained, but still, you can see the age: threads are pulling out from it all over the place. I keep my eyes on the ground and my vision fills up with feet, and I remember as I'm taking off my shoes that I have to wash up. Most of the men here are in their forties, and they've brought their kids with them. Then there is a scattering of FOB-looking dudes who talk energetically amongst themselves. It begins to plop snow outside, and now the door is opening and closing more often and the volume begins to increase. I make my way to the bathroom to wash: I follow the old man next to me as he washes; while he moves smoothly after years of practice, my motions are stunted and lag behind him. I realize that no one is paying attention to me, but I feel guilty and I want to perform everything correctly. Maybe there is salvation in this—maybe there is a reason for following things the appropriate way, for doing things the way that millions of people have, for generations and generations. Maybe the ritual movements can ease the pain and rigour of daily life and move me towards something. I am blessed with this luck right now, to be in this moment, this series of events—Anna's death, the RCMP, Hussain—that are all for me, are all to lead me here.

I say Bismillah. Nothing happens.

I dry my hands and feet and neck and face and leave the bathroom, following the old man into the large hall.

Most of the men are lined up now and facing the wall. Small rugs have been placed down, and talk is slowly ceasing. Where are they getting their rugs from? I spy a bunch of rolled-up ones in the corner and take one, unfurl it, and stand behind it as they do. The rest of the men have lined up after something in Arabic blasts out and the imam takes the lead and starts up. I'm at the left corner, so I've got people in front and to my right, and it's easy to follow because I think most people have their eyes shut and they start moving instantly, murmuring, their lips mumbling in unison. I stop thinking—I follow the body movements, my hands near my ears, my knees crackling as I bend down, touch my forehead to the floor.

I never prayed for Anna. I never spoke directly to Allah and asked Him for anything for Anna, said please this or please that for her, even at the height of whatever I thought was her illness. Our bodies bend in unison, and the murmured prayers pile up on each other in a constant hum.

I feel a little strange looking straight up at the mosque ceiling; I think it's about time I outgrew the idea that Allah is a dude sitting on a cloud watching us. That they would be up there together, watching me. The man behind me burps. Everything that I had thought was simple makes me laugh—I had gotten everything wrong. Anna was not simple; she was hidden. Whenever she threatened to show me her hidden side, I stuffed it away with a joint or a drink, or reminded her that she had a bottle full of benzos sitting in the bathroom.

What was I doing? She did not have to listen to me. She did not. I am being stupid by taking the burden of Anna's death on like this, with God watching, in His house. Her death is keeping me locked in the moment. I could forget her. This guilt webbed together the events of my life, but I don't need it to survive like I thought I did.

When Anna found out I did a small stupid thing, like when I broke into a convenience store when we were together—not really broke in; the door really just had to be shaken hard, and they mostly stocked cigarettes, newspapers, day-to-day minutiae—she waved her hands at me and repeated that she did not want to know. That was all she said: I do not want to know. Even though she already knew, because I told her, in one sentence, everything that there was to know. Each lottery ticket I scratched was a bust, not even five dollars, but by some miracle, $125 was left in the cash register. The store had a small display of fake gold chains and I stole one for her. It was thin and would break easily, but she kept it. She squeezed her eyes shut and pretended not to hear, and when I handed her the chain she did not ask where it was from.

She sold the necklace. She said it burnt her neck. I don't know who she could have sold it to. I told her she was allergic to cheap metal; that was the burning sensation.

Our bodies move like part of one machine. Each body movement is a gear. I love it the best when their hands move to their ears as if they are straining for better listening. Everyone does everything together. My body strains when I mimic the motions.

I've never seen bodies like this, all connected and working

together, without touching or talking to each other. I don't know if I could join them. They are automatic, moving with their own personal history within the singular ritual.

My chatter is slowly pressed down by prayer. All I ever needed was a place to take a breather from everything. I needed quiet without accessing my inner self; I needed quiet without asking how my own apparatus was built. The steady stream of voices are a cord that will not break, all bodies in the same direction, all bodies with the same goal. Kevin wants me to insert myself into this like a virus.

The hum is softening, and I open my eyes to see if the prayer is stopping or if it will begin again, for another movement, like a piece of music.

The bodies have stopped. The clot loosens and people start moving in different directions. Do I want to stop committing these small crimes? Matthew warned me and that was not enough. His example was not enough. I had expected all my life for another path to open up for me.

Friends start chatting and others are moving to the front, slipping on their shoes and getting ready to leave. I don't know what to do—how do I approach someone here? How do I talk to someone? I try not to look panicked and the imam has disappeared and everyone else looks like a normal person: Who am I supposed to approach? What instructions has Kevin given me? I make my way to the entrance and slip my shoes on, careful not to linger; I don't want to look like a weirdo—those are the instructions I think that he gave me specifically: Don't look like a weirdo. My shoes are on and I'm out the door with my bonkers heart, the rhythm of the prayer movements slowly dissipating from me.

Kevin calls when I'm in bed with Kali's laptop breathing quietly next to mine. I finally plugged it in and charged it. It's silver and sleek, a better model than my HP one. It's a beautiful MacBook, the ethereal essence of class. Kevin wants to buy me breakfast and we meet at Sunshine Grill.

How did it go?

What you mean?

How was it?

I didn't do anything. I prayed. I felt a stir—of God.

What? What was the mosque like?

Fine? It was fine?

Were there a lot of people?

Of course there were.

Did you notice the imam?

Sure.

Did you get his name?

I thought you told me to go and observe.

Did you notice anything?

Like what?

Did the imam speak?

Of course he spoke—he prayed, he—

Did he say anything in English?

Not to me.

Nothing?

He said a few things—he introduced. I don't know. I wasn't paying attention.

You weren't paying attention?

I wasn't paying attention? I was praying. I was nervous.

You have to do better.

Do better at what?

Kevin looks at Ryan, who sighs and groans in combination and leaves the restaurant. Kevin is quiet while he examines me. When he speaks, his voice is soft and that rough, scraped tone he had been using before is gone. His shoulders slouch. He's good at this—I can't tell where the fake-cop affectation begins or ends. I realize that he is young, just now cracking into his thirties, and he must be some sort of a good-kid protege. I'm an asset for a career move.

Do you speak Hindi? I ask.

A little. A little Arabic.

Are you Muslim?

No.

Not since nine/eleven?

My parents are Guyanese.

You know Mohammad is in your name.

Family friend I was named after.

I thought everyone was worried about the Somali Muslims now.

They've all got problem people. He looks at me to see if I have any more questions. What are you doing?

I don't know what else to tell you. I don't want to be here.

This can be a decent job.

It's weird to think of this as a job.

Working for the police?

I wouldn't be a cop. It's different than that.

What?

Snitching?

Omar. You're twenty-seven? What are you doing with yourself?

Yo, I have a dad, relax.

Why can't you be part of something? You have a bad situation—

It feels a lot like you're creating this situation.

I didn't make you rob anything. You're too suspicious. You can't see the hand trying to feed you.

It doesn't feel right to be sneaky. Doesn't this fuck you up?

No. There is a clear distinction between helping and not helping.

And this is—

Do you think you can get people in trouble if they're not headed for it?

Why does it have to be me?

Why did you break into the house?

I can't let this be a job ...

Don't involve your feelings. Where else are you going to get a hundred and twenty-five dollars a day?

A job that doesn't involve me fucking up Muslims and brown people?

You don't care.

You sent me to a mosque!

And you saw God?

I saw people minding their own business.

You're complicating this.

I don't know anything about that place.

There's a lot of kids like you.

What's that mean?

I'm here to help. It's an opportunity. It's about what you can know. He sounds like he's reading from a pamphlet. Neither of us are into this meeting. Kevin has bags under his eyes I've never noticed. He doesn't stop fidgeting or rubbing his fingers together. Have I not noticed this, or has he always been coming undone? He seems like a stray thread.

I don't have thoughts on the Middle East—not real thoughts.

Are you happy with what's going on there?

No one is—it doesn't mean that ...

No one is. You're right. We're all trying to help. He waves sheets of paper in his hand. He pitches it again as a kind of government job. I do wonder, briefly, if it comes with dental. He has no time for my arguments. He recoils at "rat," and "snitching." They mean nothing morally compromising. You don't owe these people anything.

I tell him I can't sell out an entire community, and his rebuff is so simple: You are not part of that community! Really, Omar. Do you have any honour in your life? Any duty? Anything you have to sacrifice yourself for?

I can't forget the way the bodies moved in unison.

Kevin reaches into his pocket and pulls out a small bundle of twenties. His hand looms over the table and he looks me directly in the eyes. Grocery money, he says, for yesterday's attempt. We'll get you on the books soon.

It was so easy for me to fall into that rhythm of prayer. There was a childhood joy that came with hearing that Arabic chanted, singeing the air. That joy was simple—I do not know Arabic. I count the bills: six.

I feel ... not great.

Get some food in you. See how you feel then. Kevin smiles. His gold tooth all the way at the back of his mouth glimmers. Instead of taking the money, I should smash his face in. I should shatter his teeth, sell the gold. I won't. I won't.

Six twenties. That's enough.

My tongue is flat on Kali's lower back now, where a little spread of brown hairs crawl. Her body tightens with self-consciousness; they look like little twigs that point to either side of her, separated by a dip in her spine, before her ass. She had lit a joint and given it to me, and my brain directed itself to this patch of fuzz after she asked me to touch her from behind, her face in the pillow, enjoying the way weed scuzzed into her body. My first two fingers are deep in her and I'm curling them the way she asked me to, my tongue licking her at the same time, drawing a line to her asshole. She tastes like body odour. Her fingers are flinching her clit and I'm about to move for a condom and she asks me to stay, almost shouting from the pillow. She cums with her ass against my mouth and pushes hard enough against my nose that I snap back in pain. She's finished. I wipe my mouth and she twists—her tongue finds me, my balls, she asks me to jerk myself off and we lie on our sides and I cum on her stomach. She doesn't mind the pool there until it begins sliding down onto the sheets. She lets me smoke weed inside her apartment, which I am a big fan of. I take the roach and re-roll the leftover weed into another joint.

How long ago did you guys break up?

I really don't want to talk about this.

I don't think we should leave it. I think we should talk about it.

A year ago? I don't know. Did I say one year last time to her? Or did I tell her the truth?

Are you okay?

Of course. It was ending for a while.

Can I ask something?

Can I stop you?

Did you know?

What do you mean?

Did you think she would—

No. Yes. I don't know. How do you?

Was she like ... I don't know. Mentally ill?

She was on medication.

Her ceiling fan is on and it whips and whips and whips above us, pushing the smoke out of the room. Her small portable heater is near the nest of our toes at the bottom of the bed. This is the perfect way to get the perfect temperature, she says, the blanket over her lower half. I think she likes the heat on her face when she cums; she still has not wiped me off her body. The smell of ammonia and bleach puffs into the air.

I think I love Socrates.

Yeah? Cool.

He's kind. I wish he had asked me to marry him before he left.

Why did he leave?

It's quick money.

Maybe he only realized once you were out of his life.

I think so. That makes me curious about him. The way he thinks. People who don't get what they have in front of them. You know what I mean? Like why couldn't he see me when I was in front of him—I'm worried now that he's asked me out of nostalgia. That it's not love but this, like, you know, this idea of me as a person or what life would be like. Not that that would be wrong or bad or anything. I think you make life out of ideas, like you have an idea and then you make it into a thing. You know? I love him.

He seems kind. There's a small photograph on her mirror tacked with tape that looks like it has been folded several times. He has short brown hair parted to the side and is wearing a purple oxford. He's smiling in the photograph, with his arm around Kali. She doesn't look as happy as he does, but I don't think she smiles widely.

She must also have a box like Anna. I ask if I can use her laptop, forgetting that I have it, that it is at my house. For an actual hour I've forgotten that I am an intruder here, that I caused her grief. She was feverish about smoking this weed—she said she felt uncomfortable in her own home.

I pick up her cellphone while she zzzs and there is no password on it. I go onto her Facebook page to see if she is friends with Owen. She is friends with four Owens but not him. I find him and add him as a friend of hers. I linger on his page but don't learn much, as his privacy settings are too high until he's a friend, and I'm too scared that Kali might wake up. I log on to my Gmail account and email myself keywords to see if the RCMP will notice me again:

toronto bomb CSIS blow up fuck parliament jihad

I feel like running into a wall. I watch Kali, passed out in that weed-assisted dead-zone sleep, her hands spread open. The joint is making her dream and she shivers like a dog in sleep. Moonlight fills the room and I notice the door that leads to a small balcony. I try the door and it is stuck firm and I pull hard and it gives off a loud wrench. Kali wakes up and watches me from bed. She wipes my cum off her stomach. I see a gash of wetness on her leg. She is dazed but orders me behind her again. From there she could be Anna—there is no reason for her not to be. They are both beautiful, but also, right now, Kali is white flesh with a wound. My hands are on her body and the thickness is wrong and the bones are in the wrong place—Anna had sharp hips—but I close my eyes. I rub my cock against her pussy until I harden and Kali doesn't say anything. Her fingers move over herself. She pushes against me and I push back, knocking into her, against the bed, my hand on her shoulder, and I push and push, her ass moving against me. She tells me not to cum in her, which I like because Anna would say the same thing, in a different way; Anna was on the pill, so it wasn't as frantic. I have no idea if Kali is—do Hare Krishnas abort?—and I don't know Kali that well, right, but I know that she is kind and here, and when she speaks she sounds so different, but she is a voice. I miss Anna like you would miss the sea, and I'm as surprised as I would be if all the water in the world vanished, or if the sun stopped showing up. It's too late. When you miss someone, it's too late.

Do you ever watch videos of the two of you?

No.

Like with Socrates, I do. I like to. He likes to watch videos of me and other men.

Are you asking me to make one?

No! No! I shouldn't have told you that. He sends me these little videos—these video diaries. From Korea. They are so cute.

Is that how he asked you to marry him?

That was over Skype.

Oh, real time.

Her flesh is still. I'm watching the way the freckles run up her forearm. She has a mole with a long hair coming out of it that she pulls on.

Do you ever watch old videos?

I don't think we have any. She was worried—about things getting loose on the internet.

The internet is scary. You know they can monitor all that stuff.

Yeah?

Like Canada's NSA? CSIS or whatever? I'd be scared if I were you.

Why me?

They monitor shit. You know they do.

Why *I* gotta be scared?

Dude.

'Cause I'm young and I'm brown and my hat's real low?

The news!

Do you think some spy is jerking off to your videos?

Don't.

What?

Don't. I'm so nervous about the laptop: whoever stole it. There's like all my photos, videos, essays. My whole life is on that thing.

I'm sorry.

For what?

Nothing—that sucks.

Whatever. It's stuff. The photos I guess Sock has versions of.

What about older boyfriends?

Whatever, right? Like, moving on. I've never had so amazing a boyfriend—except Socrates—that I can whatever, let go, you know? You should watch old videos. If you're still not sad.

Sure.

Kali asks me to leave because she needs to sleep early. On the way home, on College Street, Matthew and Sylvia are at the lip of Kensington, and Matthew is in clothes I've never seen him in, an outfit, a dark red pea coat like pig's blood, black jeans, shoes that point, and he's speaking to Sylvia and fiddling with her scarf. She has her heels on. Their clothes rhyme. As I walk closer, his hands quicken their pace around her neck and finally tighten the scarf to its end.

Matthew.

You okay?

I'm fine.

I offer a small smile that I split between him and her, and I walk away. I can't tell if Matthew says something to me, but I know Sylvia reaches her hand out, and I twist away from it. Matthew is awkward and Sylvia offers me a small smile that belches pity. She's trying to hide it, but it's so loud, the way she then looks at the ground. Matthew does not know what to say; I don't know what to say to him. I want to tell him about the cops and ask him what I should do, but I can't. I want to tell him I went to a mosque like he suggested. That same rage from the bar fills me and creeps into my limbs, and I know it's wrong, but you cannot stop a motion like that, except to leave, to run away. I don't know what I want to do to him. They have stopped, expecting us to talk, but I don't, I keep going, I cross the street, and go and go.

I call Emina. The phone rings too many times without going to voice mail, so I give up, but before I hang up, she answers. I ask if I can drop by quick, and she says it's late, but yes, sure, please, come over for a tea, of course you can. Her voice is warm, and when I leave my house, the snow is screeching wet across everything, that lifeless, thin, snow that drenches everything and disappears. It falls all over me and on top of the hard, dirty snow already on the ground.

I knock on her door twice before realizing there is a doorbell, and she answers in jeans and a thick sweater.

Darling. Come in.

No, no, it's okay—I have something.

I spoke to Bernie last night.

That dude tells stories, hey?

Darling. I have the kettle on.

I gotta go, actually, my kettle—my kettle is on too. I can't look her in the eye. I stare at her shins, and the long shadow behind her of her boyfriend.

Are you sure?

The wet is freaking out: snow, snow, snow.

Here. I hand her a photograph that I took from Anna's room of the two of them, arms around each other, their bodies pressed sideways tight. I got this from Bernie. From Anna's room. The photo is folded and a crease splits it down the middle. She really loved you, and it was in a box, so I figured, you know ... I don't know when they would go through the box.

Emina takes the photograph and she looks at it and I try to look at her, but she's bright, so, so bright in my vision, and she pulls me in for a hug, but I stop her.

I'm cool. I'm wet, you know.

I can't tell if it's surprising that Kali's MacBook has no password. Matthew always says white people are too trusting, but this MacBook thing makes no sense. Doesn't everyone have a password on their laptop? My jaw still clangs from Hussain's swing, and looking at the aluminum coat of Kali's computer brings that throb back. When I open the lid it goes directly to the desktop and there is a tidy arrangement of folders: *4thYear, Misc, TV, Movies, Music, Photographs, Documents.* The background is a family photograph. Her mother has her head shaved. Cancer? Hare Krishna? I peer closer to see if I can see fuzz or if the head is skin-shaved, but the resolution on the photograph isn't good enough. I click on *Photographs* and they are separated by year, going all the way back to 2008. I click on *2014,* and there are ten folders. Some have film photographs that have been scanned, but most are shaky digital photos. There is a folder titled *Socrates,* which has portraits of him, sometimes with her, often not. They are the clearest photographs that I see, composed with a clear, delicate care. The photographs here are rarely blurry, and if they are, they are for effect. The blurriness renders them panicked, like Socrates is trying to escape the eye of the camera. I keep navigating through the different folders of family photos, friends, and click on a folder called *00*, which is an array of nude photographs.

The photographs are numbered. The first photograph is of her almost clothed—her panties off but her bra on. She spreads her legs in the next, then touches herself. Kali looks like she's in his room. An amber light flows over her, and the photos are frantic. They don't have the composition of the clothed ones, and she has a smile that I recognize, her "sexy smile," she called it, the one she would use and then laugh at herself for. Kali has a fringe in these—her hair is long and reaches to her neck. She spreads herself for him again, the focus of the camera on her face. She's familiar in these, but the hair, the smile, the spread legs—not the same person, as if she saved these looks for Socrates. The second-last photograph is of her on her knees and her hand on his cock. The last photograph is unexpected. Kali and Socrates in the mirror, Kali holding the camera to her stomach, pointing towards the mirror. Socrates has his arms around her from behind and he is kissing her on the ear.

I text Matthew and ask him to come over. While I wait for his reply, I flip through the remaining folders and find two other white dudes, not named. One folder is almost twenty naked photos of some dude, but they are all missing the vividness with which she captured Socrates. I right-click on the mirror photo and read the time stamp. It was taken six months ago. They are in love.

I move to Chrome and discover Owen has accepted Kali's friend request on Facebook. Kali has left it logged in. For half an hour I click through his profile, looking for evidence of Anna. I go through his profile pictures first and find group photographs, where I recognize friends: James, Lindsay, Anna. They're from three years ago. The rest of his page has almost no information, and she never posted on his page, except on his birthday, and once, when he announced he won a scholarship, she posted a simple heart. I'm looking for a residue of her but find nothing. He has his phone number listed publicly, and his email address, and I type both into my phone (Matthew still hasn't texted me back; I've texted him twice more, it's two a.m.) and unfriend Owen from Kali's account. I need to find out where he lives.

Kali beckons me over, asking if we can have a talk and promises weed. A bottle of red wine feels like a necessary glug. It's on the round black table Kali keeps on her balcony. Her feet in my lap. She had asked me to pick up a merlot. I spent ten bucks I'm not sure I should have. I paid in change. Coins always feel fake, and I never get over the thrill of buying something that can alter me so much with quarters and dimes. The balcony is shoved full of plants and she names them out for me. They are dying in this cold air and she articulates their scientific names slowly and then follows with what she's nicknamed them. Her toenail paint is chipping. Today is mild and she asks if she can save them, even as all their leaves are aching towards the ground. Kali fills her glass and puts the bottle down next to a pack of Belmonts. I take a coin out of my pocket and pass it in between my fingers, and when the craving for a smoke gets too strong I place it in my mouth and suck it, let the bitter metal fill me up.

Have you guys, like, set a date?

No. He wants to wait. 'Til the bar is open.

So he's keeping you warm.

Don't be rude.

He sounds ... I don't know.

I wanted to maybe do this master's. In Surrey. Like, England. In environmental psychology. I can't get a job here. Like an adult-person job.

So?

So? He's coming back. The bar.

You can be his busboy. Get tip out.

I didn't expect to say yes. It shot out of my mouth.

You said—

I know! But I didn't expect him to ask. It was like. A reflex.

It's kind of mean to say no, I guess.

Did you go to school?

A semester of chef's school.

You didn't love it?

I shrug. What about, you know, if there's an after Sock?

Can you think like that if you're getting married? Like, that can't be how you go into it.

You can be a mature student everyone hates.

He told everyone in his family. I told my mom!

You can change your mind.

I've mentioned Surrey for years. It's fine. Forget it.

We can talk—

No, no. It's whatever.

Kali gets up and kisses me, unbuttoning my shirt. She runs her hand over my chest, to my belly button, and back again, and laughs to herself. What is this? What colour is this? You're always changing in the light. Is this caramel? Cocoa? Let's go in.

I have an eye sideways, glancing at Kali, unsure of her motivations. In her room, she tugs on her turtleneck and looks at her breasts. She lifts the collar to her nose and smells herself. When I look at her I don't know what I'm supposed to do: Am I supposed to sit with this pain and let it become me before I can throw it off? I look at her turn to tend to a plant and I see the way her abs twist under that sweater, and I can taste the tangy current that runs through her body and for a moment pain is far away somewhere else, sitting in a corner, but you can't hold time like that. She feels like the sun bearing down on me full blast, like she came out of a fugue dream to get me to ignore my problems.

You're really sweet, I say.

Thank you.

Thanks for everything.

It's okay. Socrates comes back soon.

Half a year. Six months. You want to end this now?

I don't know. I think so.

There's no need.

I don't know.

I know, I get it. I get it. He did it on Skype, though.

He's going to do it again when he gets here!

That's important. I wish the sun was here right now.

Do you ever miss Anna? That was a long thing.

I do. I do. So what?

I'm just interested. Sorry.

Why?

The memory of Anna's mouth, her little soul, burning through me.

I don't know. I'm trying to get to know you.

You feel bad.

No. I mean. You knew what this was.

I didn't realize an e-proposal would end it.

Don't be mean.

Do you want to talk about Anna?

I don't know! I don't know a lot about you. And now we're about to—

When did you start needing to know about me?

Don't get upset.

I'm not upset. You have a fiancé. Why are you asking me these weird questions?

Because we're friends.

We ain't friends. You bored as fuck.

Don't be stupid.

I can hear the neighbours bass pounding in slow strokes.

Kali's going through her wine so quickly it doesn't stain the glass.

You're drinking fast.

I am not.

Look at this shit—you're almost done.

You don't want to talk about Anna. Okay. I thought we were friends.

I thought we were fucking. You just said.

And we manage to be friends, too, somehow.

Yo, we don't even really know each other. It's okay. You don't have an obligation to me.

Her hands on my knees. This can't be comfortable.

I'm fine. You're good. She's sitting on me, facing away, twisting once in a while to kiss me.

After, my cum slides down my belly, onto the mattress. Her hand is still around my cock, softly now. She's made a ring with her index and thumb. Her hand to her and two fingers pulling inside her—she swivels against herself until she cums, biting my shoulder.

Can you dump Socrates?

Her jaw doesn't drop, but she turns her head to look at me. Neither of us knows if I'm joking. There is no motion to her face, her muscles steady under all that skin. I envision peeling back that topmost layer of skin to see the flesh ripple react underneath, to know that the thing I said had an impact. A blade so sharp it wouldn't hurt, or leave a scar. I'd love to read that red flesh like you would an inkblot.

No. She moves her head as she says this, shaking it from left to right. Are you being a dummy?

I mean, you could just end it. I shrug and say this with a lilt to make it clear that I'm joking, not that I am trying to staple myself to her happiness. I squeeze her sides and she laughs: a clear, uninterrupted flow, and she looks skyward towards heaven when she does—You're so sweet. And I make my way up her neck in three close kisses and taste wine on her lips. I am joking, really. It's a silly, frantic idea. Just a quick email. The right emojis would do it.

Let's stop this now.

Because he comes home so soon.

I think there should be some space before he gets back.

I want to stay.

I have an opening shift.

She doesn't let me kiss her when I leave. I'm drunk. I take a small potted plant from her garden.

I wait until the sun squats low and then go for a walk and call Kali, figuring she'll snap back for one last fuck before calling it off for good. I stop in front of her house, looking through the window at a girl in the lower apartment cutting vegetables, the basics for a soup—celery, onion, carrot—and dropping them into a pot. I have nothing prepared—I'm not really ready to say anything if she does pick up the phone. I look up at her bedroom window and see nothing; I can see her swaying from a rope around her neck, around the barrel of her fan. Is the fan turned on or off? Again, I see her: this time, oscillating with the fan, her legs hitting items on the desk, slamming against the bookshelf, the contents of her room everywhere. What about her in the bathroom, drowning on water the same colour as wine, her wrists slashed, a deep wound down the centre of her body. Or gurgling lifelessly in the froth of the toilet. I never imagine it peaceful, in bed, with a dollop of sleeping pills advancing through her body. I wonder if I'll be able to imagine us together. I will try: in the future, on an angry, unfocused night, home alone, I'll remember Kali and how she refused me grace. The past will thrum with the future. It makes me angry that she will continue to live on with me in my dreams. I wanted so little from her: just to be held steady.

I call again: it's picked up, hung up, all of it an accident.

I'm walking away from Brunswick, with the scars and scrapes of Christmas lights guiding my way. I'm not sure where to go. I see something sway quick up a tree and from the corner of my eye it looks like a giant lizard, one of those slithering dragons my father told me patrolled his childhood, the ones still populating his dreams. It's not that, of course; it's one of the fat beasts of my childhood, a raccoon. I came close to seeing my father cry once. The tears ballooned in his eyes but did not fall. It was when he told me about a casual kiddish cruelty. He used to watch lizards monitor his house, moving from closet, to wall, to under the bed, to wherever there were gaps of darkness. One day his best friend, Ankith, gathered several of the house's lizards into a bucket, took them outside, and crushed them one by one with the heel of his foot. A playful laugh tumbled out of the kid's mouth. My father didn't stop him, he didn't know why, and even though he had always loved observing the lizards, counting how many he saw in a day—fifteen was his highest count—he couldn't stop Ankith, couldn't even try. Finally, he looked away, and he looked away while telling me the story. Tears bubbled in his eyes without dropping. I can't remember why he told me the story. I watch the raccoon climb up onto a branch and move to a house. It stops to watch me.

The next day I check my phone for Matthew and instead am greeted with four texts from Kevin, asking me to go down to the mosque before a prayer time, to go and see if we can do the next thing. I'm lying in my bed, watching a sun that looks like sculpted butter hang. Snow is falling, almost wet, yellow; it's almost hot out.

What's the next thing? I ask him if it will be done after this, if I'll get left alone, and he ignores the text, instead tells me to call him when I'm down there. I don't bother shaving or changing. I have no clean underwear; I look for coins for laundry but have none. I get into yesterday's dank boxers, spray some air freshener on my socks from the day before, and slip outside the door. Maybe I can hit Kevin up for some more money after.

The wind is savage and my fingers hurt trying to get this Boston cream into my mouth. There's a guy at the Spadina and College streetcar stop with his dick out, pissing! He's drunk from last night, I guess. For the first time in a month, I can step back and appreciate Matthew, that he's been there for me, but it comes with a vehement anger. I can only appreciate him now because I know that he's spacing out from me. I miss him. I miss the warmth he brings into a room and his steady presence.

Kevin tells me to go inside and be as nervous as I want—I don't expect that. He tells me to explain my situation to whoever asks, without lying but omitting the Kevin part. Stick to the truth. I'm a lost Muslim. I have no idea what I'm doing. I'd like to get involved again. Aren't these things true? Don't say you are angry at the West. Don't mention politics. Mention you are political. Don't mention any beliefs. Don't mention the Middle

East. Don't mention Saudi Arabia. Don't mention Syria. Don't talk about anything like that—not yet. Don't be so bait. Don't mention politics! If anyone talks about politics, listen, make eye contact, don't mention your beliefs. What do you think about Syria? Who gives a shit? Say you don't really know, that it seems fucked up. Don't swear. Don't have a belief beyond: it's unfair. If someone asks you directly, deflect. Say: I don't know much, it's unfair. These are the two things you are allowed to say, and that's only if you've been asked. If you've made eye contact. Be eager. Learn. Be clean, be eager, be cool.

I take my shoes off and go to the bathroom for wudu, but it's too early; I'm here at a weird time, one of the first for prayer. Someone is rolling a few leftover rugs and putting them to the side. I see a poster board that I hadn't noticed last time and pore over it: community notices. Nothing extravagant—offers for tutoring, rent, et cetera. The dude who was rolling the rugs brings out a broom and begins sweeping. He has a long beard and is wearing a white salwar kameez that is dirty at the bottom. He looks like he's mumbling to himself. I hope he'll be able to tell me if Anna is in heaven or hell.

Do Muslims believe in ghosts?

Excuse me?

Are you the imam?

No. Do you need help?

I think so—I don't know? I'm new here?

What are you looking for?

... A mosque?

Yes, okay, you're in the right place for that! He laughs. I laugh too.

Is the imam here?

Not right now, no. He will be back later.

Can you help me?

Are you Muslim?

Yes.

Good.

I'm lost! I've drifted. I need guidance.

Yes.

Spiritual guidance.

So.

I don't know.

Are you from Toronto?

What?

I mean: do you have a family mosque?

Oh—no.

Maybe we should wait for the imam. He will be able to help you with what you're looking for. If you want to pray—you can come anytime.

I want to pray.

Prayer times are there—he points to a board that has them scrawled on it—or you can google them. Come during those times. You can speak to him after.

Should I come a little bit early?

Come a little early to clean, and then yes.

Is there like ... a group thing? Like a group thing where I can meet people?

There's an event listings board there. He points to the board I was examining earlier.

I want some community.

Okay. Prayers start shortly. You can meet an imam and talk to him about what exactly you might want.

Uh, okay.

I look around: Where do they keep the women? There are two white converts; they must have white women somewhere. Someone else has left a pair of Jordans at the front. They are toothbrush clean.

Are there imams so dumb that they would ISIS rant downtown? I watch someone peacock in. Kevin has not been clear on his instructions, so worried is he that I will fuck this up. I didn't bring anything to record. Even so, do I give him the goods right away? I have to trickle out information, at least until they ask me to record the sermons, and dole it out slowly enough that I can turn this into a job. The man strokes his beard while watching over the gathered. We make eye contact and I smile and he nods in reply. More and more men arrive and are patting each other on the back and shaking hands.

What if there is a sleeper cell in this mosque? Do I have to join?

Those Js: I can't stop thinking about them. How does he keep them so clean with the snow and slush everywhere? They have to be worth two bills. At least. No one seems to be paying any specific attention to them. Who leaves shoes like that out? They teach about God, that He is always watching us. He must take the mosques off His list, right? I do a quick scan: none of the other shoes are good. Mine are nice. Not that nice, not sneakerhead nice. Would the Js' owner have noticed them? No. Prayer starts up and bodies move. If I took the shoes and left now, everyone would know it was me, but everyone here looks vaguely like me, and I don't think I could tell them apart in a lineup. I can make up something that the imam says and get some space that way. It'll have to be something small that keeps Kevin fed. A morsel to suggest I'm improving in usefulness.

I describe it to myself easy. I need to eat. Double-dipping is fine. No one will get caught. Cops won't care about sneakers in a mosque. I can sell the shoes, which could net me at least a quarter of rent. I'll tell Kevin I'll grow one of them Taliban beards, take the job serious.

I leave the bodies. I clutch my stomach to vaguely pretend I'm sick to whoever might be watching. The pretending shifts as I eye the Js, and pain blows through my stomach. I slip on my Air Max and see that someone has put their shoes in a plastic bag. I take the plastic bag off so I can stuff the Js in them. Wait. Is there lightning suddenly outside? No—God is chill. God is chill. I'm about to scoop them when I can't breathe. I'm only sweat all of a sudden. My hands are trembling wild and I'm crinkling the bag and too scared to see if people can hear me. The noise is booming off the walls. Am I breathing? It hurts when I try. I bend over towards the Js, but I feel dizzy—shit. I'm going to faint. My stomach churns and my sweat is gushing out of my pores, my armpits, forehead; the back of my knees are swamps. I take a deep breath, just to see straight, and the sharp air helps a little but not really. I feel wobbly, as if I might fall over. It feels like a million alive things in me fighting for space. Is that just me? It's pulling my stomach in different directions—mostly out my throat, but also out my chest, like a hand inside, yanking my guts. All the bodies are moving together behind me. The doors are noisy, remember. Be chill and be quiet. You can't rob someone this nosily. I'm trying to breathe, focus, ground myself into this moment. This is everything you need: Kicks, God, Money. Be calm. I'm too scared to see if people are looking at me. My sweat is already cooling, and I'm shivering. The shoes. Fuck. When I look at them, my gut menaces me. I leave them, fuck, I have to, fuck—and vanish out the door.

I'm confused, deflated. The light hasn't changed outside: it's still blaring bright. I could have used that cash. My sweat is freezing now. What was that? I'll need Kevin's cash now. I call him:

What happened?

Nothing, really.

Wait, is it prayer time?

I guess not.

You didn't look it up?

I guess not.

You moron.

Yo—I'm not a fucking spy! This is ludicrous.

I don't want you to be a spy!

You haven't even paid me for real! Grocery money! And for what! You want me to infiltrate a mosque!

Don't be so dramatic.

(   )

What happened?

Nothing. I talked to some dude and he seemed weirded out.

What did you do?

Nothing. I asked a few questions.

Were people there?

Not that many. I mean, it's not a prayer time, I guess, right?

You fuck-up.

Whoops.

Did you meet anyone named Ifthikar?

I didn't ask anyone his name.

Did you talk to anyone young?

This dude was like forty.

Did he have a long beard?

They all had beards. This guy was cleaning.

You spoke to the caretaker.

He was the only friendly one, you know? Open vibes.

Omar, do you think this is a joke?

I did what you told me.

What did he say?

He told me to come back. He told me to look in the hallway and at the event board and to come back.

What was on the board?

I didn't really look at it?

What?!

You told me not to act suspicious.

He told you to look at it!

You told me to be cool. You want me to go back inside?

No!

I'm just outside.

Outside where?

The mosque.

You're calling me from outside the mosque?

You told me to call you when I was done.

Jesus. Kevin hangs up.

I think I'm finally ready for sleep. I lie on my bed, sinking into the mattress, half-assed creeping on Owen's Facebook from Kali's account. I shouldn't have unfriended him so quick, but I got scared. I see that Matthew is a mutual friend of theirs—Matthew knows Owen. This is weird. I hadn't noticed this before. Matthew! I send him a text to which he does not reply, so I send him four, and call him twice. He replies by text and insists that we meet up in the daytime, which I pretend to have no problem with, but I do: I don't like seeing him so early, the café windows blinding, the light thrown through the windows making me squint and shift in my seat. I don't tell him why I want to meet, but I know he's worried.

A blade of sunlight is lying on Matthew's neck while he tells me about Sylvia. He tells me the same thing that he has been telling me the last few times we've met—that he's really enjoying her—and he says that she pushes him, pushes him in a new way, in a way that isn't irritating. He tells me about the job he got at Flight Network, answering phone calls and helping customers with their bookings.

You've never really travelled, though.

Nah, man, I googled a few places before I went for the interview. It's easy. I'm the Southeast Asia specialist. Not a lot of people have been to Burma—it's easy.

I'm unsure what to say to him, unsure, almost totally, where our friendship connects anymore.

He asks me how I am, if I've found a new job, and I don't tell him anything about the RCMP, but I ask if he has a hookup at Flight Network, and he evades the question, telling me that he'll look into it, but that he has to work there for longer before they'll trust him with referring someone. Anyway, he says, you don't have any experience in the field.

All good. I think I got a link.

Yeah?

Government thing.

Damn, that's bank. Doing what?

Just ... shit. Not sure I want to.

Still. That's good benefits. He doesn't bring up Kali.

My coffee is an eight-ounce Americano. The rage in me has curdled, but I can't look at Matthew for too long. When we met up he was already sitting, so we didn't dap, shake hands, touch. The café is long and spacious, with a high, high ceiling, but it's not enough space for me and Matthew to be in the same room. It feels like we have passed the in-between state of falling out; we were good, now rotten. I don't know how to figure it out. I know he did not want to tell me the news about the note, might have regretted ever getting one, but it was fact, and he only told me out of loyalty. My anger cools with the realization that Matthew does what he thinks he is obligated. He apologizes, looking at me. Everything could be fine between us.

We haven't chilled in a while. He says this.

I know.

I'm sorry, about—

Bro. I can't.

You okay?

You know that dude, Owen?

Who?

Dude who dated Anna for a minute?

From, like, two years ago? Yeah.

How?

I dunno.

You Facebook friends.

He added me after the funeral.

What?

Weird, yeah.

Where he live?

What?

I wanna go talk to him.

Why?

'Cause he probably got a note.

Dude. Leave this.

Fuck you, man. You got a note. You were *just* a friend, and you got a fucking note. Hand-delivered by Bernie.

Matthew has nothing to say to this. He looks at me and fiddles with his teaspoon. I watch as he licks it clean of milk and coffee, and I know two things: that I'm full of a deep, permanent, gratitude for him, for his kindness, a type that I've not recognized before—and that the well of my spirit is too far gone for him and his way. I love him, but it means nothing, because I don't know what to do with it. Our paths have become misaligned.

I dunno, dude. He lives in Little Italy.

You know his address?

Nah, man.

Take a look. See if there's, like, an old party invite or something.

I gotta check.

Check. Text me. Thank you.

I tell Matthew that I have to go, that I'm sorry, I can't be here anymore—on my way out the door, I touch his shoulder and squeeze forever. Matthew sits still, his mouth open, his thoughts interrupted, and he lets me pass meekly.

Kevin keeps calling for me. Three times. I watch the phone buzz. I have to confront it. He leaves a voice mail, and I think he even uses the word "naughty." They think the mosque is a dead end for me now. I oversold the lack of action. I think they're also surprised at my inability to handle simple situations. He wants to meet across the street at a Timmies. I head down the stairs and into the cold. I'm wearing sweatpants and a coat loose on my shoulders.

I explain to Kevin again how it went, how nothing really happened. I am exhausted from meeting with Matthew; I am exhausted from only eating Mr. Noodles today. Matthew was kind enough to pick up the coffee.

That's it?

That's it. I don't want to do this.

What are you going to do for money?

What am I going to do for money? Get a job? I don't know. It takes at least, like, three months for a landlord to kick someone out.

Don't be a moron, Omar. You're floating through life.

Fuck you.

There is a small joy, like squashing an ant, in making Kevin mad. I have nothing to offer. I can't hang out in the mosque and pray and pretend to be a good Muslim, or a bad Muslim, or a turned Muslim, or whatever. I don't have the ability to do this.

What about Hussain?

What about Hussain?

Do you still talk to him?

I shouldn't be surprised he brings him up.

That dude punched me in the side of the head—no, I do not.

Can you?

What do you mean, *can* I?

Can you talk to him? We want you to talk to him.

I don't want to talk to a dude that recently clapped me on the side of the head.

Every time we have this argument, Omar, the result is the same.

Kevin, please.

If you don't want that ... then what? Then what do you have to do? *You have to work with us.* You're part of our team. Hussain has started selling computer parts alongside his wholesale clothing business. He has a lot of family in Pakistan, and we think he's going to be headed there soon to look into opening up a factory.

A bomb factory!

No, a T-shirt mill.

Oh.

He's going with his brother.

Are we not allowed to have businesses now?

Kevin slides a photograph over the table.

Do you know this guy?

Legit: no.

He's working with Hussain.

Are they part of a sweatshop empire? I could get behind squashing that.

You want to get out of the mosque?

I think you want me out of the mosque.

You want to help?

It's important to be part of society.

Meet him. Apologize.

For?

The fuck-up.

Being punched.

Tell him you have a thing.

You want me to apologize for getting punched.

You want him to meet one of our people—Saif. Saif is a connect to Lashkar-e-Taiba. Saif wants to hook him up with an opportunity to sell motherboards, with a portion of the funds going to them.

Who are they?

They're a Kashmiri terrorist group. We know they're affiliated with Al-Qaeda and maybe already in communication with ISIS.

Kashmir?!

You know we've seen his conversations online, in the open. We think we can get him on this.

He's not going to fall for this. He doesn't give a shit.

You'd be surprised.

I really don't think he gives a shit about Kashmir.

The arrest will be good for you and good for me. Hussain is a good target for this.

The dude robs Asian kids for Yeezys.

Have you watched the videos he sent you?

Sure.

And?

I've known Hussain since we were like ... fourteen. He thinks this shit is cool. He wants to be—I don't know—useful, or something. He doesn't give a shit about Kashmir.

And you are going to give him an avenue to be useful. We need you to vouch for our guy, and you need to convince Hussain that it's okay. We've got some background—

I don't vouch for this dude and I don't think this is okay.

Hussain is right there. He has a fork, right? In his path? Would a good person choose the wrong path?

I don't want to lead him down this path. This is involving me way too much. Who is actually your guy?

He works for us, like you do.

Hussain is not gonna go for this.

You think he doesn't want to feel good? To be part of something bigger than him?

I don't think he wants to fund a terrorist group.

If he doesn't want to, he won't.

So, I just ask him?

Be persuasive. Show him the door is open.

This dude is high out of his mind right now playing Xbox.

I'm sure he'd like a more constructive life.

If I don't?

If I can't get an arrest, this operation shuts down. Funding goes away. There's no reason for us to tell the cops to back off you. There's no need for you. The cops will do their thing. Kevin's voice tightens. He's speaking so fast to me now, actually asking instead of telling. We need this to keep our project going and to keep money, for you, to keep coming in.

How can you arrest him for an idea you give him?

I think of the men in the mosque, their bodies moving together towards Mecca, their prayers going to different imaginations of the same God. I didn't know them. It didn't matter.

I can't keep giving you money if we're getting nothing back from it. If we're going to work together, as a team, we need this arrest. It's right for everyone.

This is like a trade. I feel weightless, as if I'm hovering out of my seat. I can see myself slack-jawed, Kevin sweating furiously, trying to make this switch happen. His eyes are focused in on me. He's made a bet that he would be able to use me for something. He wants his reward.

Hussain has a capability deeper than yours.

I can't ... Fuck, man.

I think about the swap. I could take over Hussain's life. His Xbox, his car, his Cassie, his kids. The pain in my head bubbles big from forehead to jaw whenever I think of him. It's as blurry as the memory of that night. I knew Hussain all my life to be an asshole, and I knew how desperate we all were to carve a path for ourselves into this country's living memory. Hussain in some crazy supermax prison, on the front page of newspapers, dislocated from his kids' lives. Him in the jail they have for terrorists, where they aren't allowed to talk to or see or, more importantly, touch their family members. It astounds me that they think

Hussain capable of organized violence. Because he shared videos of violence in Syria?

There is an appeal to Kevin's logic: if Hussain wouldn't, he won't. Am I really this responsible for Hussain's choices? The heat in the room is enormous; Kevin sweats bad. He wants this so much. Am I really responsible for Hussain's future? I know what Hussain would do. I know what silky sentences Kevin would tell me to feed him and how to appeal to his thirsts: for fame, for money, for charity. They are the thirsts we all have. Kevin would make it easy for me. I want so terrifyingly for my life to be on a path I recognize. Hussain would take this. He would imagine selling the motherboards, he would imagine giving to the Kashmiris, he would think twice about nothing, he would boast.

I can't.

Don't think. Kevin brushes off my response. Fuck Hussain. I need this. We'll get you something organized after. Think of yourself as a middle man. Your contribution is important—don't think it's not—but it's not as vital as what Hussain will actually decide. He's doing this to himself. You're just opening a door.

Why need me then? You don't need me.

I feel sick, my body screaming at itself. Fucking Hussain and his dumb gold chain necklace. I know the responsibility Kevin is offering me is false. I hate Hussain's shitty fade and his North York drawl, the way words fall out of his mouth instead of being spoken. I need air. I need cold air and the sun breaking on my skin. I can't do that. I can't do this.

I can't do it.

Kevin lays his hand on mine and squeezes.

I have to go. I gotta go.

Think this through, Omar. This is nothing. This is barely an ask. You know what this means if you go? Kevin does not raise his voice. He lets go of my hand and pain from his clench spreads across me. You know what my next call is—who comes to you next?

I can no longer look him in the eye. I look out the window for somewhere to go. What would Anna want? It's a stupid question. I try anyway to conjure her advice, and nothing comes up. I can't imagine her speaking to me.

Do what you gotta do, dude. I can't ... do this to someone.

I know this means cops at my door. I know that one action of mine might not be more correct than another, and that nothing I do now redeems what I have not done previous. I know, finally, what my body could do, and what it could not. I am fine with him going to jail, but I cannot send him there.

Omar. I need this.

I'm out. I'm out. I can't do this. Call who you have to.

Omar! You don't give a shit. This is nothing. You know he'll do it.

So let him do it, man.

I need your help.

I can't.

You don't give a shit about him.

I get up from my seat while Kevin looks at me. It feels like something has tugged me down onto the earth and for two seconds I can forget my mistakes.

The air cools and I breathe it in, and out, and I walk, unable to look at Kevin and unable to hear him, his words pouring into my ears like gibberish, and I say, over and over, it's fine, it's fine, it's fine.

I'm sweaty when I leave the Tim Hortons and look at my phone. Owen lives on Palmerston. I have to move fast, before Kevin calls whoever he calls. I cringe when I hear sirens, afraid, but I take a deep breath—it won't be dramatic like that. Probably just a calm knock on my door. Matthew has texted me the full address. I take a shower when I get home and sit on the couch, thumbing through TV channels, trying to control my heart. I have to move fast, but I have to wait for the sun to drop. Once it does, I slide on my shoes and out my door.

The house has been sectioned off into units: one in the basement, I think, one on the main floor, and then one upstairs. The front door has a handwritten sign that says, *Come in through the back!* on eight-by-eleven paper. A smiley face. I walk along the side and into the backyard, and the gate opens easily to three people talking with cigarettes and *X*'s marked on their hands. It's a small party so far, but it's fattening. It's nine p.m. You have to pay to get in and I give up five bucks and get a black *X* across on my hand too.

I see him right when I get in, in the kitchen. He is about two inches taller than me and has close-cropped brown hair and a white girl he's pulled in close to his chest. Their skin blends together. He kisses her on the nape; she is almost chest high on him, blonde, wearing jeans and shitty-looking knee-high boots. She's the only person—except me—who's kept their shoes on.

I move past and into the hallway. There's one bedroom at the far end and a study adjacent. In the bedroom there's a photograph of him and the girl in a frame on the dresser. The bed is tidy, with a heap of coats on top. They are ruffled on top of each other, about ten jackets, and I resist the urge to go through the pockets; then I give in, digging through the topmost jacket—a really nice Canada Goose one—and am sad to find no money. The room is painted a suave red and the bedsheets are a bright green. I thumb through the planner on the dresser: hers. Charlotte. I close the bedroom door and then open the dresser drawers: panties, socks, both of their underwear mixed together. His is on the left, rolled in tight balls, and hers is heaped on the right, a splatter zigzag of colours. I can feel bass through the closed door. I open all the drawers one by one and find nonsense. No paper. I look in the closet, where his shirts are. None of her clothes in here. There's a shoebox on the top shelf that I open and it's full of bureaucratic documents: a passport, et cetera. Her clothes are in a box on the floor. Maybe this is a housewarming for her moving in. There must be a keg somewhere if they are charging five bucks.

Hey, man? Owen is at the door.

I'm knee-deep in his closet. I've turned on the bedside lamp—this scene looks believably sketchy. He doesn't look angry but confused; his face is reddening.

Omar?

Yo, Owen.

Omar? What are you doing?

I step back from the closet. The box is in my hands. He doesn't look like he wants to fight. He looks at the box, looks at me, takes a step inside the room, and shuts the door. His face is flushed.

Omar, man, what are you doing? I haven't seen you in ages.

Do we know each other?

You're Anna's ex?

Sure.

Dude, we've met.

Oh, sorry—bad memory.

What are you doing?

I'm looking for Anna's suicide note.

What?

I'm looking to see if Anna left you a note. Sorry yo, this is weird.

Are you drunk?

Nah, not at all.

Good.

Are you?

A little. I'm also, uh, a little high. I'm sorry if I'm talking weirdly.

I paid. I show him the *X* marked on my hand.

Cool.

You moved in with your girl.

Last weekend. Charlotte.

Congratulations. That's good.

Thanks.

Did she leave you a note?

She did.

Yeah?

It's like a page.

Can I see it?

I don't think it's for me. It doesn't have a name on it. I don't think it's for me.

What do you mean? Where is it?

It's like two pages long ... I didn't read the whole thing. Fuck. It's like two pages long. I didn't read the whole thing. It was intense. I'm sorry.

Okay.

I couldn't read the whole thing. I started to—but. Man. Are you okay? Are you sure ...

Yeah, yeah, I'm good.

It was like two pages long.

Yeah, I got that.

It was handwritten.

Why don't you give it to me?

It didn't say a name, dude, I swear, it said—*For you*, or something.

Okay, cool yo, where is it?

Her dad gave it to me at the funeral.

Bernie?

He gave it to me after the funeral and Charlotte was with me and I started to read it on the bus because I was like—okay this says bye or something; we dated, but for like, how long, you know? And I read like a paragraph and I could tell it wasn't for me. Like, for sure, it wasn't for me. This thing was intense.

Okay.

I was reading it and was like, whoa, dude, this shit is not for me. This letter is not for me.

Yo, cool, great. Give me the letter!

It was super intimate. I mean. I read one paragraph. But Charlotte could see—I got red in the face.

Okay.

Was it for you?

Yeah, dude, what the fuck you think?

I'm sorry.

That's cool. That's cool that's cool that's cool that's cool.

Dude.

It's fucking fine, man. Where's it at?

I don't have it.

(   )

I don't have it. I threw it out, man.

(   )

I threw it out. I got out at Bloor and I threw it out—I kinda panicked. I panicked. I panicked. I'm sorry.

You threw it out where?

In the garbage, at Bloor station.

Like, the subway?

In the subway.

Yo, what? Why?

I don't know. I was like ... this isn't for me. This isn't for me. I started shaking and Charlotte was kinda freaking out. I told her that Anna was my friend, you know, it wasn't a big thing. I mean, it was a thing, but like ... so small. I met her parents once, I guess, and she was like, This is my boyfriend, and then a week later she kinda started curving me and stopped answering my calls. I called and ...

Owen is on the bed and, I think, crying. He is sitting on the lump of coats. I remember touching Matthew's shoulder earlier in the day and how much transferred with that small feel.

What happened with you two?

Nothing, man, we had a bad night and got super wasted and had a huge fight. That was it. I didn't do anything, but she was gone. I mean, I yelled at her, but I was drunk—I don't remember.

When was this?

So long ago, man. Two years ago? Ages?

There was a night she came to my apartment in the rain, drunk, soaked cold. She was ruined and screaming and banging on my door. And she was smashing against my door and woke me up and this guy named Emerald was living with me and she woke his ass up and screamed at him to get me. Emerald was a good guy and he let her in and she was wet and shivering and she fell asleep on my floor in a little ball after I got her clothes off and put a blanket on her. In the morning, she was gone. After that night, I kept my ringer on when I went to sleep. She never got that drunk and came to me again.

Was it raining that night?

I have no idea.

What happened?

Nothing. I messaged her on Facebook once or twice, but she was gone. She ghosted. She was gone. What was I going to do?

Why did you get that note?

Her parents. She introduced me as her boyfriend.

(   )

Dude, I'm so sorry.

So you threw it out?!

Dude—I didn't like ... I'm sorry.

Fuck off.

I'm sorry.

Yeah.

Maybe they still have it.

Who?

Bloor station. The TTC.

Did you throw it in the trash?

I did.

Then why the fuck would they still have it?

The sky looks clawed open. I have to imagine the stars, all the constellations hovering above, behind the field of pollution. I call my father and tell him that Anna died, and he is drunk and says, Good, at least she's in heaven, and then he asks me if she would have gone to heaven. I move down Brunswick and walk across lawns where my footsteps are quieter, and I feel translucent, as if I am ready to invisible myself and float up into the air.

I wonder what the note said. I wonder if it was an accounting of our daily activities, like cooking eggs for dinner, late-night texts, early-morning coffees, her crying into my shoulder, me having someone I could be quiet with. I wonder if mine was the last note she wrote, or the first, or maybe it was the tossed-off one that she couldn't write much for. I knew in front of Owen that it didn't matter. That in some essential way, being so greedy for love had meant that I couldn't see her, that I never knew her, that my thirst for her was more vicarious than my knowledge of her, that my greediness had more depth than the space I gave her to live.

The snow has nearly gone from the ground, and the grass is dead. Or it's yellow; I'm not sure if that's the same. It looks orange under these street lights.

Kali's laptop is under my arm. I'm worried; maybe I should have wrapped it in something to protect it against the cold. It's okay, though—I can't leave it outside, anyway; someone will steal it. She's close enough to College Street that anyone could wander up and snatch it up.

I put the laptop down on the Welcome mat. I ring the doorbell, wait, ring it again, and turn down her stairs and go off towards Kensington. Maybe Matthew will have time for me tonight.

Photo: Magida El-Kassis

Adnan Khan has written for *VICE*, the *Globe and Mail*, and *Hazlitt*. He has been nominated for a National Magazine Award, and in 2016, he won the RBC Taylor Emerging Writer Award. *There Has to Be a Knife* is his first novel.